MY ENEMIES MY FRIENDS

JOHN STANKO

urbanpress

My Enemies My Friends
by John Stanko
Copyright © 2018 John W. Stanko

ISBN # 978-1-63360-085-0

For Worldwide Distribution
Printed in the U.S.A.

Urban Press
P.O. Box 8881
Pittsburgh, PA 15221-0881 USA
412.646.2780
www.urbanpress.us

CHAPTER 1

Pastor Harold Portis had come to his church office to work on his Sunday message and prepare for his next seminary class, but his mind was on anything but those two projects. In a few minutes, a delegation of deacons was coming to pay a visit, and it was not a social call. Issues had been simmering in the church for quite a few months, and Pastor Portis knew they were probably coming to let him know a vote was scheduled concerning his removal as pastor in the coming weeks.

How had things gone so wrong? Harold wondered. Pastor Portis and his family had moved to the Pittsburgh area five years ago from Buffalo, New York to pastor

Three Rivers Baptist Church located east of the city. At first, things had gone well, as is common for most new church appointments. People were friendly and there was much excitement as Harold's family got settled into a new home and new schools. The vote to bring Pastor Portis was almost unanimous after Three Rivers had been without a pastor for nearly two years. During that time, the pulpit had been filled with visiting speakers and two other candidates had made multiple visits, but no invitation to pastor the church had been extended to them. Then Pastor Portis came, and the congregation felt they had found their man.

Pastor Portis was 36 years old and a graduate of Word of God Bible College in upstate New York. He had pastored part-time while he worked to support his family as a software engineer – a job that paid the bills, but nothing more. Harold had felt a call to ministry since he and his wife had gotten married when he was 24 and she was 22. They had two children, Nathan who was 9 and Sharon who was 7 when they moved to Pittsburgh. After Harold completed his degree, he hoped to transition into the ministry and Three Rivers seemed like the perfect fit.

Three Rivers was a black Baptist church founded in 1927. The church had a sanctuary that seated 950 people, but only about 200 were in attendance when Pastor Portis assumed the role of pastor. The church experienced slow but steady growth over Harold's five-year tenure so that Sunday morning worship now numbered about 350 in two services. The youth ministry had grown, as had the children's ministry once his wife Lois assumed leadership there. Lois was also a school teacher in the Pittsburgh Public Schools, and her gift of working with children had helped the church grow.

Soon after Harold came to Three Rivers, however, there were signs of trouble instigated by some of the old crowd. The first confrontation was over what Harold came to label the "music wars." The church had consumed a steady diet of traditional hymns over the years, but Pastor Portis decided to change that. He introduced an earlier Sunday morning service at 8:30 AM that was geared toward a younger crowd, and that included more contemporary Christian music as opposed to hymns. Even though the older crowd did not attend the earlier service, they did not like what they heard about it – people lifting their hands and clapping with no "opening the doors of the church" altar call at the end of the service. Pastor Portis wanted those attending not to feel like the purpose of the gathering was to get those present to "join" the church.

Then there was more tension when Pastor Portis cancelled the annual pastor's anniversary celebration. He felt it consumed too much time and effort, time that could be devoted to community outreach and ministry to the neighborhood as expressed through the church's weekly feeding program and food bank. Pastor Portis felt he was sufficiently paid so that between his salary and his wife's, they had no need of an anniversary bonus. That did not sit well with some who felt like all the other churches had a pastor's anniversary event. It just didn't seem right not to have one after 90 years of tradition.

Some people complained, but others left the church. More would have left, but Three Rivers had a historic cemetery on the church's property, and many members had ancestors – grandparents, great-grandparents, uncles and aunts – who were buried in the graveyard. They weren't going to leave Three Rivers unless they could take their family with them, which of course meant they weren't leaving.

There were meetings and confrontations, rumblings and grumblings as Pastor Portis continued to make changes. Many people supported and applauded the changes, but some vocal critics did not and began to express their disapproval in various ways. Some confronted Pastor Portis after his sermons on Sundays. Others phoned or emailed their comments. Still others expressed their anger at the changes by withholding their offerings and tithes, and some just stopped talking, which meant they walked right past Pastor Portis and his family without so much as a hello.

The final straw came over the portable altar that sat on the floor in front of the pulpit. The altar was made of blonde wood and was about the size of a magician's box that would hold an assistant who was about to be sawed in two. The wooden box was on wheels, but it never went anywhere, no matter what event was taking place. The only time the altar was used was when the ushers counted the offering in full view of the congregation, which was another throwback to how things had been done many years ago. Other than that, the box sat there as it had for generations.

Pastor Portis had wanted to move the so-called altar permanently, but of course had met stiff resistance, especially from the older saints who liked the thought of having something that seemed so spiritual – an altar – like other churches had. Finally, Pastor Portis had the altar wheeled over to the side of the church front, and the church was abuzz when people showed up for the first Sunday service after the move. Some cried, some left, and others made a beeline for the pastor's office to express their shock and disapproval.

Up to that point, the deacons had several meetings with Pastor Portis, revealing that they were as divided as the church membership over the changes he had made. The altar for some was the last straw, and they began to lobby the membership for a pastoral change. Since Pastor Portis had been voted in by the congregation, it would require a congregational vote to remove him.

The campaign to remove him became intense, and some of the younger deacons decided it was time to leave Three Rivers altogether, which swung the balance of power toward those who favored Pastor Portis' removal. Once they were confident they had the necessary votes among the deacons, the opposition turned their attention to the congregation, which was also divided. With more people who had no stomach for the politics leaving the church, the opposition deacons were confident they were close to having enough votes for a simple majority to remove Harold.

Harold was not making much progress on his

sermon, but he did open the box that contained the textbooks for his next class at Tri-State Theological Seminary. He was pursuing his Masters of Divinity Degree and his next class, which started the following night, was on the book of Psalms. He was looking forward to the class, as he did all his M. Div. classes, but at that moment, his thoughts were on the group of men who were headed his way, this time not to discuss what was going on with the church, but to talk about his future at Three Rivers.

★★★★★★

The men began to arrive at 6:30 for the 6:45 meeting, but no one proceeded to the pastor's office until everyone had arrived. Pastor Portis could hear them milling about in his secretary's area. Finally, when the head deacon, LeRoy Robinson, arrived, the nine men knocked on the door and entered the office. Pastor Portis greeted them warmly for he truly loved those men and still believed they could work out their differences. At the same time, he felt God had sent him to lead Three Rivers Baptist Church, and he was determined to do that, trusting God to preserve him since He called him there.

Deacon Robinson opened the meeting and asked for a word of prayer. Deacon Johnson volunteered to pray, and the men bowed their heads and closed their eyes, assuming the usual prayer position. Pastor Portis, known for his humor and light-hearted approach to ministry that had made him a favorite among the youth of the church, decided to close only one eye, keeping the other one open to watch *and* pray, just in case. After prayer, the meeting began.

"Pastor Portis," Deacon Robinson began, "we have had more than a few meetings with you to discuss our differences and the direction of the church. We've chronicled our displeasure at the changes you've made over these last few years." The other deacons listened and nodded their heads in agreement.

"We're good Baptist people, and some of the changes we believe have taken us away from our Baptist traditions into modern trends that are disturbing for us," Deacon Robinson continued. "We have an obligation to our forefathers who built this church to maintain and preserve those traditions and quite frankly, Pastor, we don't feel that is happening under your leadership."

Pastor Portis had a lot to say, but he felt like he had said it all in previous meetings. He had determined to listen rather than turn the meeting into a debate on his leadership style or decisions. "Go on, Deacon Robinson, go on," is all that Pastor Portis could think to say.

Deacon Robinson complied. "Therefore, Pastor Portis, we've come to explain that, under the bylaws of our church constitution, the deacons have voted to hold a congregational meeting to decide to retain or remove you from the position of pastor at a special meeting of the membership on Sunday evening, three weeks from tonight, August 28 at 6 PM." Deacon Robinson studied Pastor Portis as he spoke, as did all the other deacons. They saw no visible signs of distress, but rather a calm that made them wonder if Pastor Portis cared or grasped the gravity of the situation. Then Pastor Portis spoke with every eye and ear focused on what he was about to say – and how he said it.

"Brothers, we've gone over again and again my reforms and why I felt they were important," Pastor Portis explained. "I see that some of those deacons who supported those changes are not here this evening. I suppose that's not important now."

Pastor Portis continued, "I'll neither defend myself any longer nor will I campaign to win the vote on August 28, any more than I campaigned to obtain this position. I'll put it in God's hands and trust His judgment. Unless there's anything else we need to discuss, I'd recommend you go about doing what you need to do, while I go about what I need to do, and that is put the finishing touches on this week's sermon."

The deacons breathed a sigh of relief, for some thought the meeting would be contentious. "Very well, then," Deacon Robinson said. "We'll notify the congregation of the August 28 meeting. We would ask that you not make any further leadership decisions, and that we all be in prayer for the upcoming session. Pastor, you need not be at that session."

"Oh, I plan on being there. Let's close in prayer, shall we?" Pastor Portis said. While he may have appeared calm on the outside, he was seething within, trying to control his emotions as he faced the fact that a referendum was about to be held on his leadership. In all probability, he would be left without enough support to continue in his current position . . . unless the Lord intervened. The meeting closed but Pastor Portis could not remember who closed in prayer.

CHAPTER 2

When Harold finished up at the office, he headed home to his house about five miles away. His children were in their rooms, but his wife Lois was eager to hear about the meeting. "How did the meeting go?" she inquired, studying her husband for clues of his thinking, just as the deacons had done.

"The meeting was short and sweet – well, probably not so sweet," Harold replied. "It was pretty much as we expected. The deacons have set my recall or vote-of-no-confidence meeting for August 28."

"What happens then?" Lois asked.

"Well, if a majority vote to remove me as pastor,

then our time is finished here," Harold explained. "If the majority votes to keep me, then I have a decision to make."

Lois asked the obvious, "What decision?"

Harold said, "The decision of whether I want to stay and lead a divided congregation or not."

Lois held back tears while she let her thoughts become audible, "And that means moving, the kids in new schools, the shame of it all . . ." her voice quivered and she did not finish expressing her thoughts.

"I know, I know," Harold responded, not really knowing what to say and not confident he could change the mood of the moment. "We'll just have to trust the Lord and see what the next few weeks bring. I'm not sure why they set the date for August 28. I should have asked for a quicker decision."

"Yes, I don't want to show up in church and act all nice and cordial while I'm wondering who's for us and who's against us," Lois said with a trace of anger. "All this over an altar that no one ever used," Lois said, shaking her head.

"No, it's more than that," Harold added. "It's what the altar represented. This is all about change and the identity of the church. I misread where they were at, and thought they were ready for the changes, but I guess they weren't, at least some, maybe most of them. We'll see if it was the majority of them in three weeks," Harold said wistfully.

"And now, let me see what I can have as a snack. I have my first class tomorrow night at the seminary and want to get a good night's sleep," Harold said in faith, for he knew that in all probability, both he and his wife would be up for a while, even once they crawled under the covers of their bed. *This is going to be the longest three weeks of my life,* Harold thought, as he opened the refrigerator, saw what he wanted, and cut himself a piece of cherry pie.

★★★★★

While Harold wanted to get a good night's sleep, it proved elusive. After Harold and Lois chatted in bed till the wee hours of the morning, Harold was up earlier than expected. As soon as he opened his eyes, his mind began to race with questions. *What will happen to us? Where will we have to go? How will we make ends meet?*

Harold figured there was no use lying in bed, so he got up, put on some coffee, and went down to the basement to his usual spot for devotions. He opened his Bible and turned to the book of Psalms, a book that had comforted him and so many others in times of deep trouble. He knew it was no coincidence that he was beginning a study of the psalms that evening in class. He began to read, choosing a random place to begin as the coffee brewed upstairs. Ironically, his attention fell on Psalm 22:

> *My God, my God, why have you forsaken me?*
> *Why are you so far from saving me,*
> *so far from my cries of anguish?*
> *My God, I cry out by day, but you do not answer,*
> *by night, but I find no rest (verses 1-2).*

Harold thought the last phrase was certainly true in his case, for he had not been sleeping well lately. He continued to read:

> *Many bulls surround me;*
> *strong bulls of Bashan encircle me.*
> *Roaring lions that tear their prey*
> *open their mouths wide against me.*
> *I am poured out like water,*
> *and all my bones are out of joint.*
> *My heart has turned to wax;*
> *it has melted within me.*
> *My mouth is dried up like a potsherd,*
> *and my tongue sticks to the roof of my mouth;*
> *you lay me in the dust of death (verses 12-15).*

David certainly had a way with words, Harold thought, as he reflected on the phrases "poured out like water" and "my heart has turned to wax." *I couldn't have found words to describe how I feel, but those words are close enough.* Harold chuckled to himself, amused that he could laugh at a time like this.

Then Harold continued to the prayer portion of Psalm 22, and he prayed it for himself rather than just reading the words as a detached observer:

> *But you, Lord, do not be far from me.*
> *You are my strength; come quickly to help me.*
> *Deliver me from the sword,*
> *my precious life from the power of the dogs.*
> *Rescue me from the mouth of the lions;*
> *save me from the horns of the wild oxen.*
>
> *I will declare your name to my people;*

in the assembly I will praise you.
You who fear the Lord, praise him!
All you descendants of Jacob, honor him!
Revere him, all you descendants of Israel!
For he has not despised or scorned
the suffering of the afflicted one;
he has not hidden his face from him
but has listened to his cry for help (verses 19-24).

Harold took out his journal and began to record his thoughts, including his reflections from the reading he had just done. He wrote out this prayer, *Oh Lord, it can't be a coincidence that I'm enrolled in a class starting tonight called "The Study of Psalms." Lord, use that class to speak to me as I walk through these next few weeks. I put my trust in You!* With that, Harold closed his journal and went back upstairs, for he heard Lois in the kitchen preparing for her day ahead, which included returning to school to prepare for the beginning of the school year. Harold did not share with his wife what he had been reading or praying.

★★★★★

The class at the seminary began at 6 PM. Harold went into the office around noon since he would not get out of class until 10 PM, which made for a long day. He had two counseling appointments and had to put the finishing touches on his sermon. The good news was Friday was an off day, and then he put in a half day on Saturday before resting for Sunday's marathon of two morning services and one evening prayer gathering.

Before his first appointment, Harold made sure he had everything he needed for the start of class. He had the syllabus printed and his briefcase packed with his textbooks. Harold looked over the syllabus again and shook his head. Since the class was only five weeks, there was a lot of independent study with a major paper due every week. *I hope I'm able to handle all this along with what's going on at the church,* he thought. The introduction to the syllabus read:

> "In this course, learners study the Book of Psalms, giving attention to the various forms of the Psalms and their function within the historical experience of Israel. The course begins by focusing on the formulation and interpretation of the psalms. Students then examine in detail the various types of psalms: lament, royal, pilgrimage, wisdom, messianic, and psalms of descriptive praise."

Then Harold noticed one intriguing class objective included in the syllabus: "Study the historical circumstances that existed when some of the psalms were created." Harold had never given much thought to that, just assuming the Spirit had inspired the psalms and writers responded by writing them. *Well, I guess that makes sense,* Harold thought. *I know I'll be crying out to God over these next few weeks, so the psalmists were probably going through "stuff" when they wrote, just like I am.*

His reflection was interrupted when his secretary alerted him that his first counseling appointment had arrived. "Thank you, Mildred. Tell them I'll be right out,"

Harold said as he checked his briefcase one last time in preparation for his evening class.

★★★★★

The afternoon went by quickly and Harold left at 5 PM to grab a sandwich before class. He had another 12 months until he finished his Master of Divinity degree, and he could not help wondering how the vote in three weeks would impact that path to his degree. Harold arrived at the seminary ten minutes before class started, and he could tell it was going to be a large class. There were already 14 students in their seats, and some were always running late due to traffic.

Harold recognized a few students from previous classes, and they greeted. A few of the veteran students were out in the hall talking, and Harold spoke with a young lady named Veronica who had been in his Systematic Theology class last year.

"How's your summer going?" she asked. "Did you get away at all?"

"No," Harold responding, shaking his head. "I've been occupied at the church pretty much. Lois is now back to school, so we missed our opportunity. But maybe in a few weeks I'll have the time to do something." Harold could not believe he said that, but Veronica was oblivious to what he was alluding to.

He had never had Dr. Bruce Jackson for any class, but he heard good things about him from other students. People who had taken his psalms class before reported it was fantastic, for Dr. Jackson gave insights and perspectives that made the psalms come to life. The psalms already played an important role in Harold's devotional life, so he was ready for them to take on a whole new meaning as Dr. Jackson walked in the door.

He was an older man, pretty much like a prototypical professor. It was summer time, so he was dressed casually, although a few of the students had on suits and ties, and Harold thought, *They must be pastors! Only a pastor would wear a suit in the heat of summer!* He would later find out that they were indeed "men of the cloth."

"Good evening, ladies and gentlemen," Dr. Jackson began. "It's my pleasure to welcome you to the beginning of another term. My name is Dr. Bruce Jackson, and I'll be your instructor for the next five weeks. I'd prefer to say I'm your facilitator for those weeks, for I'm here to help you grow and learn as we study the book of Psalms together. You'll have a lot of work to do on your own, for this class is short. Therefore, you'll be reading and then helping me teach the class with presentations of what you've learned from your own studies."

Harold liked that thought: *Dr. Jackson is a facilitator. He's going to guide and oversee my learning, but God is the One who will direct and make it happen – with my cooperation, of course.*

"Let's begin by introducing ourselves. Take about five minutes and tell the class who you are, a little about what you do and where you do it, and what you hope to gain from the class," Dr. Jackson suggested. There ended up being about 20 students in the class, an almost even mix of men and women. Seven were African American, and twelve were pastors, able to take the course because it was a five-week intensive toward the end of summer. *I wonder if any of my classmates know of any job openings,* Harold wondered with amusement.

After all the students had spoken for more than an hour, Dr. Jackson provided information on his background, which included serving as a pastor, missionary, and seminary professor. Harold thought it interesting that Dr. Jackson had served as a pastor. "These five weeks are going to go by quickly," Dr. Jackson explained, "but I've found that immersing yourself in the psalms for five weeks is like taking a plunge into cold waters. It's refreshing, but startling at the same time. Because we have so little time together, let's begin."

Having said that, Dr. Jackson led the students through the syllabus, pointing out the highlights and his expectations for the next five weeks. "You'll notice there are four books for this class," Dr. Jackson pointed out. "We won't read everything in those four books, but I wanted you to have them in your library. Once you begin to study the psalms, it can become a lifelong practice," Dr. Jackson continued. "I know, because that's what happened to me. As you continue your studies, these books will prove to be invaluable."

"Does anyone have any questions?" Dr. Jackson asked, pausing for a moment. "If not, then let's begin, ladies and gentlemen, our study of the book of Psalms!" Dr. Jackson announced, ready to move on. Harold liked his style.

CHAPTER 3

Before Harold knew it, the four-hour class was over, and it was a breathtaking ride for the entire evening. As he drove home, he could not wait to discuss what he learned with Lois, who he knew would be up and waiting. It was their custom for Harold to sit and share what he had learned in class with her so that she could participate, even though at home with the children.

As Harold drove, he wondered to himself, *Why didn't I know these things about the psalms? How could I have read them for so many years, but been oblivious to many aspects of what makes the book of Psalms unique? Why didn't I know more about the book as a whole instead of just focusing on individual psalms?* Harold thought of the line from the movie *Forrest Gump*, when Forrest said, "Momma said life is like a box of chocolates. You never know what you are going to get!" Harold had been treating the Psalms like a box of chocolates, picking out this one or that one according to his taste and need. Tonight, after only one class, he knew he would never approach the psalms like that again.

As he parked in the garage and came upstairs, Lois was sitting at the kitchen table, working on her computer. "How was class?" she asked, not looking up.

"Lois, my life changed tonight! I've never had a class like it!" Harold gushed. That caused Lois to look up to see if he was serious, and she could tell by the smile on his face that he was.

"Then tell me, tell me all about it," Lois said, as she prepared a new document on the computer where she could take notes, as if she was in class.

"I will as soon as I get something to eat," Harold responded. "Is there any of that pie left from yesterday?" Harold answered his own question by opening the refrigerator and seeing one piece all by itself and covered in plastic wrap. "That pie looks like it has my name on it!" He made some tea, uncovered the pie, sat down at the kitchen table, and opened his computer to read from his notes. "Okay, where do I begin?"

"From the beginning, Harold, I want it all," Lois exclaimed. "With what's going on with us, I need to hear what God has to say to us from the book of Psalms," and with that, their kitchen classroom session began.

★★★★★

"All right," Harold began. We started out the class with this book," and Harold pulled out *Encountering the Book of Psalms,* "but we looked at bits of information from all the texts." Harold then spread them out on the table.

"The first thing that struck me was the variety of the psalms," Harold said, taking on the air of a teacher as opposed to a student. "Some of the them are prayers, some are worship songs, and others are poems." Lois began to type, capturing what Harold was saying. "We don't know for sure, but probably some of the psalms were for Temple worship with instruments, perhaps even an orchestra of sorts!" Harold could not contain his excitement. "Some were individual psalms, spoken and written by one person, but others were corporate psalms, sung or recited by a group with a message that contained 'we' pronouns as opposed to 'I'.

"For me, the psalms have been mostly for personal enrichment and devotions, but many of the psalms were made to be enjoyed and appreciated in the context of corporate worship," Harold added. "That was something that blew me away tonight when I saw that, but there were many things that blew my mind tonight. I didn't want the class to stop."

"It hasn't," Lois pointed out, "it's still going on!"

"Good point," Harold said, affirming Lois' comment, "but please raise your hand if you want to speak," Harold joked.

"Yes, teacher," Lois responded mockingly.

"Then we got into some technical stuff, using words like stich, distich, tristich, strophe, and parallelism," Harold continued, Lois stopping him for the correct spellings. "Many of the psalms are poems and were constructed and composed with great care but also great creativity."

"The main point was that the psalms are often written using parallelism, which means the author stated an idea in one line, and then focused more closely on the idea in the second line." Harold waited for Lois to finish writing before he continued.

"Sometimes the parallelism is synonymous, in that the second line continues or completes the thought in the first. At other times, the parallel is antithetical, in that the idea in the second line contrasts with the first." Lois raised her hand as she had been instructed to do.

"Can you give me any examples, professor?" she said in a high-pitched, girlish voice.

"Well, Psalm 27:1 would be an example of synonymous parallelism: 'The Lord is my light and my salvation – whom shall I fear? The Lord is the stronghold of my life – of whom shall I be afraid?' Do you see how those two lines keep the same theme, the second completing the thought of the first?" Lois nodded her head.

"Then for an example of antithetical parallelism, let's look at Psalm 20:7-8: 'Some trust in chariots and some in horses, but we trust in the name of the Lord our God. They are brought to their knees and fall, but we rise and stand firm.' The second line contrasts the statement made in the first line."

Lois commented, "I never noticed or realized that. Tell me more," but Harold stared at her, and she apologized. "Sorry, professor, I spoke out of turn."

"That's okay, but don't make a habit of it," as Harold took a bite of pie. "Let's move on."

"The real thing that blew me away tonight was when we got into the author's advice to read the psalms through multiple perspectives, but let me explain before you ask," as Harold anticipated Lois' need to ask a question.

"The author made the point that there are six experiences that we need to consider as we study a psalm. Six, Lois, not just one. Don't ask me what they are, I'm going to list them," he again preempted an incoming question. "The perspectives are:

1. The psalmist's experience

2. The editor's experience

3. The reader's experience

4. The apostles' experience

5. The literary critic's experience

6. The student's experience."

"What stunned me tonight, Lois, and made a deep impression was that the psalms were edited! Someone had to collect and select them, and then put them in a specific order, and these editors did so with purpose. Not only are the psalms the inspired word of God, but the *order* of the psalm is inspired. The book has a message in its totality, not just in the message of the individual psalms." Harold stopped to let that sink in – and he was still relishing that insight himself.

All Lois could say was, "Wow! Please continue."

"We'll talk more about the editors later, and I need some more time to research and learn about that, but let's look more at number six, at the student's experience," Harold directed. "Since you and I, and any reader for that matter, are the 'students,' the author came up with six questions we must ask as we examine or read any psalm. The goal is to 'determine, to the extent that is possible, the historical/cultural setting of the psalm.'"

"That sounds a bit technical or contrived to me," responded Lois.

"I think it's worth looking at," Harold responded, "so let me give you the six questions, and then let's see how much more we can cover tonight. The six are:

1. **Who is speaking in the psalm?** While 73 of the psalms are credited to King David, there are also psalms written by Moses, Solomon, and others, though we are not quite sure who those other authors were (the sons of Korah, for example).

2. **Is this psalm personal or corporate?** Some of the psalms were for personal reflection, prayer, or devotion, but some were written in first person plural (we) and were meant to be sung or recited in a group setting.

3. **For what purpose was the psalm written?** Some were pure praise, but others were written to complain to God about current affairs.

4. **What was the emotional orientation of the psalm?** Some of them were written in great distress

and others in great joy.

5. **What is the genre**? This is just a fancy word for the type of psalm it is, and there are many such categories, such as hymns, laments, thanksgiving, expressions of confidence, psalms of remembrance, wisdom psalms, or a psalm to honor the king. (Dr. Jackson said the list of genres can vary from one commentator to another.)

6. **Is there a recurring refrain or words in the psalm?** Our songs today have refrains or choruses that repeat after the verses. The psalms had the same thing and those refrains reinforced the main message or conclusion of the psalm.

"These six questions help to slow the readers down so that they can examine a psalm more closely and reflect on its full meaning," Harold added.

Lois commented, "I can't believe all you learned and covered in the first night. How exciting!"

"Yes, and we went over so much more. I can hardly wait to go over my notes and sit in the next class," Harold said with schoolboy enthusiasm. "But right now, this student has got to get some sleep. Class is over for tonight!"

★★★★★

Class was so good that Harold forgot about his troubles with the church, but he awoke the next morning with the thought, *In a little more than two weeks, what am I going to do? What will happen to us?* He looked over and Lois was still asleep, and he could hear that the children were as well. It was just a week till school started again, and he wanted them to sleep in as much as possible before then. He quietly slipped out of bed, put on some coffee, and went into the basement to sit in his favorite recliner.

"Well, I don't just want to study the psalms, I need them to speak to me over the next couple of weeks as I approach the day of the vote," Harold said out loud to no one in particular as he went upstairs to fix his coffee. As Harold settled back into his chair, he turned to one psalm that had caught his eye in class last night. When he found Psalm 3, he read,

Lord, how many are my foes!
How many rise up against me!
Many are saying of me,
"God will not deliver him."

But you, Lord, are a shield around me,
my glory, the One who lifts my head high.
I call out to the Lord,
and he answers me from his holy mountain.

I lie down and sleep;
I wake again, because the Lord sustains me.
I will not fear though tens of thousands
assail me on every side.

Arise, Lord!
Deliver me, my God!
Strike all my enemies on the jaw;
break the teeth of the wicked.

From the Lord comes deliverance.
May your blessing be on your people.

Harold decided to apply what he had learned last night to Psalm 3 by applying the six questions.

1. Who is speaking in the psalm? Harold had never paid attention to the headings on some of the psalms, but the heading for Psalm 3 is "A psalm of David. When he fled from his son Absalom." Harold turned and read the story of Absalom's betrayal and David's response in 2 Samuel 15. It occurred to Harold that David had (or took) the time to write a psalm when he was going through his family problems, and that psalm had helped millions down through the ages. That encouraged Harold not to allow his current dilemma to keep him from focusing on the Lord and helping other people, even though he was in pain. He recorded that insight in his journal: *Jesus ministered to the thief next to Him while He was on the cross. I need to maintain my ministry focus over these next few weeks. There are many who are going through difficult things just like I am, and I need to be open to how I can help them.*

2. Is this psalm personal or corporate? This was obviously a personal psalm containing David's testimony about God's faithfulness despite his troubles. Harold wrote in his journal, *I won't blame God for my troubles. God's in this with me! Also, I'll have a testimony when this is all over.*

3. For what purpose was the psalm written? This psalm was a cry for help against David's enemies. It was also a psalm of faith or trust in the Lord. Harold recorded, *David's candor is shocking. He asked God to break his enemy's jaw! Who is my enemy right now? How honest can*

I be with God? How honest should I be?

4. What was the emotional orientation of the psalm? This grabbed Harold's attention, for David had been in a state of anxiety and despair when he wrote. In his agitated state, David talked to the Lord and asked God to wipe out his enemies! *The Bible is a book of love,* Harold reflected, *but David was sharing raw emotions with the Lord and those emotions called down judgment on his foes. I'll have to come back to that one later,* and Harold wrote down a question in his journal so he could ask it in class if the occasion arose: *If the Bible is a book about a God of love for enemies and forgiveness, what place does a call to harm enemies have?*

5. What is the genre? Harold had not yet mastered all the genre, but this one seemed like a lament, especially after Harold looked up the word online: "a passionate expression of grief or sorrow." Harold wrote, *David took everything to the Lord. He didn't pray religious prayers or say words he thought he was supposed to pray. He was transparent and open.* One of his textbooks said that a lament contains a "complaint against God, against an enemy (the problem is external), or the psalmist's complaint against himself (the problem is internal). When Harold went back to Psalm 22 that he had read yesterday morning, he saw that it had an example of all three laments: God, others, and self.

6. Is there a recurring refrain or words in the psalm? Harold did not see any recurring words in this psalm, but he sensed a recurring theme: suffering, prayer, and dealing with enemies and opposition. He wrote those in his journal.

Harold was going through a difficult time with his enemies, or perhaps he should label them his opponents. In his mind, he had done what was best for the church long-term, but people resisted the changes, and vilified him in the process. Yet he had to keep in mind that the people in his church were not his enemies, as Paul had taught:

> *For though we live in the world, we do not wage war as the world does. The weapons we fight with are not the weapons of the world. On the contrary, they have divine power to demolish strongholds. We demolish arguments and every pretension that sets itself up against the knowledge of God, and we take captive every thought to make it obedient to Christ (2 Corinthians 10:3-5).*

Harold could understand the resistance, but he could not understand how personal the opposition had become. There were those who shared their concerns over Harold's leadership with his wife, and others openly campaigned not only to stop the changes, but to remove him. It had become hurtful because Harold had completely misjudged the intensity of the feelings about the changes he had instituted, especially the portable altar that never moved. He thought people would come around and understand.

Then when attendance declined, the money declined with it, and that riled up some of the deacons who had been supportive. Now there was what seemed like a full-scale battle going on, and it was painful to watch and experience. Harold had considered resigning, but as he prayed, he felt he was supposed to see this through to the end. The psalms class could not have come at a better time.

Harold heard his children stirring in the kitchen, so he knew it was time to end his devotional studies. He had promised to take the children to the zoo before school started again, and this was the day it would work out to do so.

CHAPTER 4

The first Sunday after the deacons' meeting was pretty much business as usual, but with only two weeks until the congregational meeting, the atmosphere was tense. A letter had been sent out to the membership, so many of the people were aware of what was going on. In truth, people had been aware of the tension that existed in the church, and of course there was talk after both services about the upcoming meeting and what it all meant. After the second service, Pastor Portis returned to his office to pack his briefcase and head home when he found a sealed envelope under his door. That was unusual, but these were unusual times, so before he left, he sat down on the couch in his office, opened the letter, and read it:

Dear Pastor Portis,

I received the letter about the church meeting in two weeks, and I am glad this issue is coming to a vote. You had no right to do the things you did with our church, a church my grandparents attended and helped build. I thought of leaving from time to time, but decided this was *my* church before it was *your* church, and it will be *my* church after *you are gone*. I regret I have only one vote to cast, but you can rest assured that my vote will be against you and your leadership. You have a lot to learn.

An angry member

Well, that's a fine way to end Sunday services, thought Harold, *and they didn't even bother to sign their name. Oh, Lord, help me during these coming weeks. I want to do Your will, even if it means moving on from here. Amen.* Harold thought of his study of Psalm 3 and remembered how David cried out to Lord against his enemies. *Oh Lord, deliver me from people who would write such a letter.* And with that prayer and insight into the reality of his situation, Pastor Portis departed the church for Sunday dinner before he was to return for the Sunday evening service.

★★★★★

Monday was Harold's day off, but he wanted to use most of it to get ready for Thursday's class. It was the first day of school for the kids and Lois, so the house would be quieter than it had been all summer. After the children were off and Lois left for work, Harold sat down at the kitchen table with his textbooks and computer to do some study.

For Thursday's class, Harold had a paper due that would discuss the general format of the book of Psalms. Before he started, he found the letter he had received in church and it made him sad to think people were that upset over his leadership. As he re-read the letter, he again considered resigning to avoid the congregational meeting. He had not told Lois about the letter, and probably would not. He felt he had burdened her enough with the matter, and she was understandably worried about their future – as was he. This letter would only serve as a dagger to her heart after they had been through so much to get to Pittsburgh and serve at Three Rivers.

Before Harold could study the psalms, he needed to find help in the psalms to restore his focus so he could read and write. As he flipped through the book, he came across Psalm 57 and as he read, it seemed pertinent to where he was at this morning:

Have mercy on me, my God, have mercy on me,
for in you I take refuge.
I will take refuge in the shadow of your wings
until the disaster has passed.

I cry out to God Most High,
to God, who vindicates me.
He sends from heaven and saves me,
rebuking those who hotly pursue me—

God sends forth his love and his faithfulness.

I am in the midst of lions;
I am forced to dwell among ravenous beasts—
men whose teeth are spears and arrows,
whose tongues are sharp swords.

Be exalted, O God, above the heavens;
let your glory be over all the earth.

They spread a net for my feet—
I was bowed down in distress.
They dug a pit in my path—
but they have fallen into it themselves.

My heart, O God, is steadfast,
my heart is steadfast;
I will sing and make music.
Awake, my soul!
Awake, harp and lyre!
I will awaken the dawn.

I will praise you, Lord, among the nations;
I will sing of you among the peoples.
For great is your love, reaching to the heavens;
your faithfulness reaches to the skies.

Be exalted, O God, above the heavens;
let your glory be over all the earth.

As Harold read through the psalm, he kept the heading of the psalm in mind:

For the director of music. To the tune of "Do Not Destroy." Of David. A miktam. When he had fled from Saul into the cave.

Harold had never paid much attention to the headings of the individual psalms, but when he took a quick look at some other psalms, he saw that many of them had descriptive headings that framed the psalm: who was to use it, who wrote it, the melody that should be used when it was sung, and the circumstances surrounding its composition. Harold decided to use those titles as the launching point for his study. He always tried to follow his interests and not a set course when studying the Bible. After he applied the six questions that helped him focus on the content and genre, Harold returned to the information revealed in the psalm's title.

This was obviously a song when it was created, wrote Harold, *for the melody was well known and actually called 'Do not Destroy'. Now that's an interesting song title!* Harold thought of John 10:10, where Jesus said, "The thief comes only to steal and kill and destroy; I have come that they may have life, and have it to the full." While it was a personal psalm, written in the first person, it seemed like it was to be sung by the congregation as the personal testimony of each singer that God was and is a preserver of life.

Harold noticed that this psalm was referred to as a *miktam*, but his research revealed that no one really knows what that word meant. Some believe it was a percussion or wind instrument, while others feel it may have pertained to a literary form of the psalm. *No need to linger there,* Harold concluded, because the real gem in the title seemed to be the circumstances surrounding it: "When Saul had sent men to watch David's house to kill him." *Now that sounds like something I can relate to!* Harold said out loud, even though no one was there.

David wrote the psalm in response to the situation described in 1 Samuel 24, which Harold took time to read:

> *After Saul returned from pursuing the Philistines, he was told, "David is in the Desert of En Gedi." So Saul took three thousand able young men from all Israel and set out to look for David and his men near the Crags of the Wild Goats.*
>
> *He came to the sheep pens along the way; a cave was there, and Saul went in to relieve himself. David and his men were far back in the cave. The men said, "This is the day the Lord spoke of when he said to you, 'I will give your enemy into your hands for you to deal with as you wish.'" Then David crept up unnoticed and cut off a corner of Saul's robe.*
>
> *Afterward, David was conscience-stricken for having cut off a corner of his robe. He said to his men, "The Lord forbid that I should do such a thing to my master, the Lord's anointed, or lay my hand on him; for he is the anointed of the Lord." With these words David sharply rebuked his men and did not allow them to attack Saul. And Saul left the cave and went his way.*
>
> *Then David went out of the cave and called out to Saul, "My lord the king!" When Saul looked behind him, David bowed down and prostrated himself with his face to the ground. He said to Saul, "Why do you listen when men say, 'David is bent*

on harming you'? This day you have seen with your own eyes how the Lord delivered you into my hands in the cave. Some urged me to kill you, but I spared you; I said, 'I will not lay my hand on my lord, because he is the Lord's anointed'" (verses 1-10).

Harold recorded his insights from this passage in his journal:

1. David's family could not avoid the implications of what David was going through, for David was on the run and away from his family. *Sorry, Lois, Nathan, and Sharon, this church ordeal is a family matter and not just about me. I know I've been preoccupied with this matter, and I'll make it up to you.*

2. David was being pursued by people he had served and helped. *David reminded Saul of his faithfulness to Saul's service, and Saul was moved for a moment, but then resumed his treacherous pursuit.*

3. David was careful to honor the authority, even when the authority was misguided and vulnerable. *David was a mighty warrior and the men and allies in the cave with him expected him to 'tear up' Saul. Instead, he brought back only a corner of Saul's robe and had conscience pangs when he did that! I must honor the deacons of Three Rivers as the authorities put in charge by God and not seek to diminish them in the eyes of the people.*

4. David had people who stood with him and they were together in the cave. *I remember that a seasoned pastor told me one time, 'Not everyone is against you; most people don't care.' I must not act like the entire church is against me. Some have expressed support throughout my time here.*

5. Pursuing the call of God presents special problems and stirs up opposition. *Opposition isn't always a sign I'm doing something wrong, but an indicator that I'm doing something right. Yet, I must face my own shortcomings in this difficult time.*

Harold was intrigued, energized, and encouraged, but he had an early dental appointment, so he broke off his study and determined to return to it later so he could finish his paper due for Thursday's class.

★★★★★

Harold was surprised by how well his paper came together as he worked on it for the rest of the week. The paper gave him a good excuse not to go into the office, but Mildred kept him abreast of anything he needed to know. He did go in for a few hours on Tuesday and Wednesday, but Thursday was the day to put the paper together, and as most students, he worked up to the last minute to get it done, discovering he had run out of printer ink, which necessitated a last-minute trip to the office supply store.

He liked to arrive early to get his mind in gear,

but as he was entering the building, he noticed a young lady in the doorway leading to the back lot with her face in her hands. The pastoral urge got the best of Harold, and he detoured to the doorway to see if he could help.

"Are you alright?" Harold asked, startling the woman.

"Yes, I mean no, I mean I don't know how I feel?" she responded.

"May I pray with you? Would you like to talk? Do both?" Harold inquired cautiously.

"Oh, I don't want to trouble you," the woman answered, but Harold was not convinced she meant it.

"Are you in the Psalms class?" Harold asked.

"I am, and I know you are too," she replied.

"What's your name?"

"Sharlene."

"And I'm Harold. Let me pray for you and then perhaps we can talk during the break," Harold suggested.

"Yes, okay, thank you," Sharlene said, as her tears and sobs stopped.

Harold prayed a perfunctory prayer since he had no idea what was going on. After he finished, Sharlene had settled down, thanked him, and they set off for class, entering just before Dr. Jackson walked in the door.

★★★★★

"Good evening, everyone," Dr. Jackson began. "Let's open in prayer and then I'd like to hear from you to know what you learned from this week's assignment. Who would like to pray?" Harold figured he had already started when he prayed for Sharlene and was on a roll, so he volunteered.

"Thank you, Mr. . .?" Dr. Jackson said.

"Reverend Portis, Reverend Harold Portis." When Harold stated his name, Sharlene swung her head quickly to the right in surprise, studying his features before she settled back into her normal posture. Harold made a mental note of her response as he prayed a prayer of blessing over the class.

Dr. Jackson continued, oblivious to Sharlene's reaction and seemingly unmoved by what Harold considered his anointed prayer. "This week, you were to do some research on the structure of the book of Psalms. Who would like to report on something you learned and why it was significant to you?"

As usual, no one responded quickly so they would not seem to be drawing attention to themselves or appear too eager to talk. *Christians tend to be more concerned about what others think than they should,* Harold thought, as he endured the awkward silence. Finally, after the usual awkward silence, a young man raised his hand and proceeded to give his report.

"Your name, please," Dr. Jackson asked.

"My name is Brandon Walborne and I'm assistant pastor at South Hills Nazarene Church," the man answered.

"Proceed," Dr. Jackson directed.

"Well, I was fascinated with what I discovered this week," Brandon explained. "I just thought the psalms were a loosely-knit collection of poems and songs, but wow, was I ever wrong! First, it seems like Psalm 1 and

2, and then Psalms 146 to 150 serve as the bookends of the rest of the psalms. The first two set the tone, and the last five wrap everything up."

"What tone do the first two set?" Dr. Jackson interrupted to ask.

"Well, from what I could see, Psalm 1 contained the theme for the entire book, and that theme is the supremacy of the word or law of God. May I read Psalm 1?" Dr. Jackson nodded his approval.

Blessed is the one
who does not walk in step with the wicked
or stand in the way that sinners take
or sit in the company of mockers,
but whose delight is in the law of the Lord,
and who meditates on his law day and night.
That person is like a tree planted by streams of water,
which yields its fruit in season
and whose leaf does not wither—
whatever they do prospers.

Not so the wicked!
They are like chaff
that the wind blows away.
Therefore the wicked will not stand in the judgment,
nor sinners in the assembly of the righteous.

For the Lord watches over the way of the righteous,
but the way of the wicked leads to destruction.

"There are two kinds of people – those who put their trust in the law and the wicked who do not," Brandon enthused. "The author and editor, who may have been the same person, were stating that the rest of the collection was going to expand on the theme that the keeper of the Law is blessed while those who ignore the Law are wicked, explaining the fate of both groups."

"Very good, Mr. Walborne," Dr. Jackson said. "Did anyone else notice those first two psalms and their significance?"

A middle-aged African American woman raised her hand. "Yes, I did. My name is Bridget Walters, and I work at Children's Hospital as a case worker."

"Welcome, Ms. Walters, and what did you discover about Psalm 1 and 2?"

"Psalm 2 continues the theme of Psalm 1, explaining that it will not go well for the wicked, but the psalm was not about ordinary people, it was about leaders and kings," Bridget commented. Without asking permission, she read Psalm 2:

> *Why do the nations conspire*
> *and the peoples plot in vain?*
> *The kings of the earth rise up*
> *and the rulers band together*
> *against the Lord and against his anointed, saying,*
> *"Let us break their chains*
> *and throw off their shackles."*
> *The One enthroned in heaven laughs;*
> *the Lord scoffs at them.*
> *He rebukes them in his anger*
> *and terrifies them in his wrath, saying,*
> *"I have installed my king*
> *on Zion, my holy mountain."*
> *I will proclaim the Lord's decree:*

He said to me, "You are my son;
today I have become your father.
Ask me,
and I will make the nations your inheritance,
the ends of the earth your possession.
You will break them with a rod of iron;
you will dash them to pieces like pottery."

Therefore, you kings, be wise;
be warned, you rulers of the earth.
Serve the Lord with fear
and celebrate his rule with trembling.
Kiss his son, or he will be angry
and your way will lead to your destruction,
for his wrath can flare up in a moment.
Blessed are all who take refuge in him.

"This psalm made me think of so many things," Bridget stated.

"Like what?" Dr. Jackson inquired.

"Well for one, I went to Ephesians 6:12, which says, 'For our struggle is not against flesh and blood, but against the rulers, against the authorities, against the powers of this dark world and against the spiritual forces of evil in the heavenly realms.' Psalm 2 informs us that there are powerful forces, in the natural and the spiritual, that are opposing the things and people of God. The rest of the psalms after Psalm 2 talk about this battle, and the implications for the saints of God, especially for leadership."

"And does the reference in Psalm 2 to 'the Lord and his anointed' and 'I have installed my king on my holy mountain' cause you to think of anyone?" Dr. Jackson was leading Bridget to an important insight.

"Why, yes, it sounds like language that describes the eventual ministry and position of the Lord Jesus!" Bridget exclaimed.

That caused another classmate to raise his hand but not wait to be recognized to speak: "Yes, Psalm 1 declared that God's word is supreme but Psalm 2 spoke to the fact that Israel was waiting for a Messiah, their king, who would reign. Therefore, the Jews were a blessed people not because they had a holy building called the Temple. They were blessed because they were people of the Law and people waiting for God's deliverer."

Harold had not thought of that insight, and he made a note to pursue that line of thought on his own time. Then he raised his hand. "Yes, Reverend Portis."

"The psalmist had indicated in Psalm 1 that the law of the Lord or word of God was to be the foundation for the righteous, and then the final five psalms indicate that praise is the other weapon those who believe are to use in their fight against the kings discussed in Psalm 2 who oppose the Lord and His appointed ruler."

With that said, another woman raised her hand, "Yes, that surprised me in Psalm 2 that the wicked were urged to 'kiss his son.' I had never seen that before, but then the more I read, the more I realized that the psalms were really about Jesus, or at least a foreshadowing of His life, work, and ministry," she declared.

"And you are?" Dr. Jackson interjected.

"Sorry, my excitement got the best of me. I'm

Yolanda Washington. In fact, the entire second psalm talks about God's response to the wicked and their lawlessness was to establish His son on the throne. Thank You, Lord, thank You, Jesus!" With that the class laughed, and Dr. Jackson added, "Report, don't preach, Ms. Washington," and again, the class laughed.

Then Sharlene raised her hand. "I'm Sharlene Fuller," and with that, it was Harold's turn to jerk his head to look at Sharlene. He had a Fuller in his church, and she resembled a woman in his church. *Could they be related?* he wondered.

"I was impressed with the basic structure of the psalms, following the theme of the first two introductory psalms," Sharlene explained. "The psalms are divided into five books, and that made me think of the Law of Moses, which is presented in the first five books of the Bible called the Pentateuch. Five books of Psalms – five books of the Pentateuch."

"Yes, it was as if the writers were saying, 'The Temple is gone, but we shouldn't have based our existence on a building that will pass away, but on the word of God, which will never pass away,'" Harold interjected.

Then another student shared that many of the psalms were compiled and edited while the Jews were in exile in Babylon. Some of the psalms had existed for centuries, but were not compiled into their five books with the "bookends" of Psalms 1 and 2, and 146-150 until the need arose.

The class went on for another hour as students shared ther insights from the assigned readings and their personal research and study. Even a random visitor to the class could have felt the excitement and energy from the discussion and reports.

After the class had finished, Dr. Jackson went on to add his insight to the discussion, and Harold found himself taking copious notes on his computer. Before he knew it, break time arrived, and since no one had moved during the discussion, everyone was ready for a break.

★★★★★

As the break began, Sharlene walked past Harold and said, "My mother goes to your church, Pastor Portis."

Harold broke into a smile and said, "I thought you resembled someone in my church. Hazel Fuller is your mother?"

"Yes, she has been all my life!" Sharlene joked, and they both laughed. What was not a laughing matter was that Sharlene's mother was part of the "opposition" at Three Rivers. She was not very happy with Harold's performance, and he wondered how much Sharlene knew about his predicament.

"Let's get some coffee," Harold suggested, and they both exited the classroom and headed for the snack area.

"So, are you feeling better, Sharlene?" Harold inquired.

"Oh yes, thank you, Pastor," Sharlene responded. "Work has been awful lately and I'm not getting along with my boss. The pressure at times is almost too much, and there are rumors a downsizing is imminent."

"Ahhh," Harold noted. "I think I know how you feel."

"You do?" Sharlene said with surprise. "I thought you wouldn't have anything like that in a church."

"Well, there are different kinds of pressures in a church, working with people and all that," Harold responded, surprised that she was surprised at his comment. *Maybe she doesn't know what's going on at the church,* Harold thought to himself. "Where do you work, if I may ask?" Harold inquired.

"I am with a consulting firm in the North Hills," Sharlene told him. "I have my bachelor's in management, but I don't think that's where my future lies."

"Where do you think your future lies?" Harold continued the conversation.

"In ministry," she said. "I want to go into ministry."

"Hummm, talk to me before you make any final decisions," Harold said, only partly joking, but Sharlene missed the sarcasm and said, "I will."

After some more chit chat that included Sharlene inquiring about Harold's family, how he got to Pittsburgh, and how long he had been a pastor, it was time for class to resume. Harold still wasn't sure what Sharlene knew, but he was confident in the fact that she knew very little, which was a relief to him. They both returned to the class and before anyone wanted it to be over, the class finished and it was time to go home.

CHAPTER 5

Lois heard the garage door and waited at the kitchen table for Harold to come up the stairs. "Hey there," she greeted Harold without getting up. "How was class?"

"It was fantastic," Harold enthused. "Wait till I tell you what we learned tonight, but also, guess who's in my class?"

"I can't begin to know," Lois said. "Tell me."

"Her name's Sharlene Fuller."

"Is she related to Hazel Fuller?" Lois wondered aloud.

"Yes, her daughter."

"Oh, that's interesting. What's she doing in your class?"

"She wants to go into ministry. She's some sort of consultant now. Doesn't seem like her mother has told her much about what's going on at the church."

"I would be careful, Harold, you know how her mother has been," Lois warned.

"I will. She seems pretty innocent, but we'll see. Anyway," Harold added, changing the subject, "tonight's class was fantastic! We learned so much and the time just flew by. Are you ready for a download?"

"That's why I'm at the kitchen table, with computer open and ready to learn," Lois exclaimed.

"I like this setup," Harold said, "we get two educations for the price of one!"

"And you do most of the work," Lois pointed out with a laugh.

"Hum, I never thought of it that way, but let's get started," Harold said. "But first, do we have any pie?" As he opened the refrigerator, he saw his favorite. "Peach pie! Yes ma'am, that's what I'm talking about!"

★★★★★

After Harold had made short work of half the peach pie, he got down to business with Lois. "Alright, we talked about the structure of the book tonight. Psalm 1 and 2 seem to be the introduction, and then the psalms are divided into five books. I'd never paid attention, but it seems that there's a theme with each book."

Lois was taking notes on her computer and she

had her Bible open on the table as well. Harold gave her time to read Psalms 1 and 2, and then she asked, "What are the themes? I'm ready."

"Well, before we go over the textbooks, let's review some history. Most people think that David wrote the psalms, but he only wrote about 75 of them. There are others written by Moses, Solomon, some are anonymous, and others are attributed to people we don't know much about, like the sons of Korah, the family of Esaph, and men named Ethan and Heman."

"I wonder if Heman was really a he-man?" Lois interrupted, not being able to control herself.

"One more outburst like that, and it's off to bed with you," Harold scolded.

"Sorry, please proceed."

"The timeline for the psalms being written is actually not during David's lifetime, but over hundreds of years!" Harold said with excitement. "The thing that has blown me away so far is that the psalms were compiled and edited not in David's lifetime, which was around 1100 BC, or BCE as it is called today, but when Israel was in exile in Babylon from 583 BCE to 510."

"Wow!" Lois said, and Harold responded, "Yes, double wow."

"That means that someone preserved the psalms for hundreds of years, carried them to Babylon, and then others had to get involved in the editing and compilation process," Harold explained. "This is an amazing story, and there's more."

"When Judah was carried into exile in 583, the

survivors were a devastated people. Their false prophets had claimed that their exile would never occur, that God would not permit it, solely because they had the Temple. They felt God needed them to maintain His house, so to speak, so even though they were acting wickedly, they believed they were going to get a 'pass' from God."

Lois typed furiously, but at times she stopped because she was fascinated by what Harold was saying.

"Then Israel was in Babylon and they were mourning their beloved land, Temple, and way of life. They were oppressed by an idolatrous people in a foreign land and had to put the pieces of their lives back together. So what did they do?"

"I don't know, what?" Lois interrupted.

"I was going to tell you if you let me," Harold said with mock irritation. "They turned to the psalms, but not just a reading of individual psalms. They began to assemble them in the order we know today, and the editors, whoever they were, tried to help those in exile make sense of the catastrophe that had taken place – and leave a lasting message of the lessons they learned for future generations."

"So, let me give you the general layout of the five books, and then the theme for each one. Keep in mind, this is my own interpretation of what each of the books stood for to the editors. Also, keep in mind that the five books emerged over the period of the seventy-year exile in response to the unthinkable that had occurred when God sent His people into exile, using a foreign, godless nation as His agents."

- Book One: Psalm 1 to 41 – Theme: "It Wasn't Our Fault"

- Book Two: Psalms 42 to 72 – Theme: "We May Have Been Partly to Blame"

- Book Three: Psalms 73 to 89 – Theme: "It Was Our Fault, but Did We Deserve This Kind of Punishment?"

- Book Four: Psalms 90 to 106 – Theme: "It Was Our Fault: God is Just"

- Book Five: Psalms 107 to 150 – Theme: "We Are Ready to Go Home!"

Each of the first four books ends with a line that summarizes Israel's response to God's work in them as a people:

- Praise be to the Lord, the God of Israel, from everlasting to everlasting. Amen and Amen (Psalm 41:13).

- Praise be to the Lord God, the God of Israel, who alone does marvelous deeds. Praise be to his glorious name forever; may the whole earth be filled with his glory. Amen and Amen (Psalm 72:18-19).

- Praise be to the Lord forever! Amen and Amen (Psalm 82:52).

- Praise be to the Lord, the God of Israel, from everlasting to everlasting. Let all the people say, "Amen!" Praise the Lord (Psalm 106:28).

"Then the last five psalms are an exhortation for all the earth to praise the Lord. Therefore, each of the five books ends with a directive for God's people to praise Him, not to build Him buildings or study His law, but to worship Him for who He is and what He has done for His people."

"Keep in mind that not every psalm fits the themes I have just described, but there is a clear progression of understanding as to what had happened that caused God to send them away. As they came to grips with their role in causing the exile, there was a progression of understanding that basically said, 'When we go home – and God *is* going to take us home – things are going to be different. We'll no longer be attached to a building; we're going to be people of the Word and people waiting for our King to be enthroned on God's holy mountain."

"How were things going to be different?" Lois could not help but ask.

"Well, this is also so interesting," Harold said, in full teaching mode. "Where else in the Bible are there five books that are considered one entire section, with each one having a specific theme?"

"That's easy," Lois replied, "the first five books of the Bible called the Pentateuch."

"Smart girl," Harold said grinning, "I married you not only for your looks but your brains," and Lois almost blushed.

"So the editors in exile were basically saying, 'We got off track before our exile. We were infatuated with a building, the Temple, but originally we were not people of the building, we were the people of the Torah or Law. We allowed our focus to wander, and it got us in trouble. When we go home, we're not going to focus on the building. We're going to have the Law as our foundation and main identity as it was in the beginning." Harold stopped and shook his head slowly as the impact of his own words sunk in.

"As I said, the last five psalms of the book are psalms of praise. Let's look at Psalm 148, one of the last five psalms in the book:

> *Praise the Lord.*
>
> *Praise the Lord from the heavens;*
> *praise him in the heights above.*
> *Praise him, all his angels;*
> *praise him, all his heavenly hosts.*
> *Praise him, sun and moon;*
> *praise him, all you shining stars.*
> *Praise him, you highest heavens*
> *and you waters above the skies.*
>
> *Let them praise the name of the Lord,*
> *for at his command they were created,*
> *and he established them for ever and ever—*
> *he issued a decree that will never pass away.*
>
> *Praise the Lord from the earth,*
> *you great sea creatures and all ocean depths,*
> *lightning and hail, snow and clouds,*
> *stormy winds that do his bidding,*
> *you mountains and all hills,*
> *fruit trees and all cedars,*

> *wild animals and all cattle,*
> *small creatures and flying birds,*
> *kings of the earth and all nations,*
> *you princes and all rulers on earth,*
> *young men and women,*
> *old men and children.*

> *Let them praise the name of the Lord,*
> *for his name alone is exalted;*
> *his splendor is above the earth and the heavens.*
> *And he has raised up for his people a horn,*
> *the praise of all his faithful servants,*
> *of Israel, the people close to his heart.*

> *Praise the Lord.*

"Lois, can you see the significance of that?" Harold asked, waiting long enough so that Lois knew he expected her to attempt an answer.

"Uh, that we should have more exuberant praise in church?" Lois guessed.

"No, no," Harold said with a frown, "the editors were saying that they would be not only a people of the Torah or Word, but also a people of praise!" Lois nodded and took notes. "Jumping ahead of myself, they went back to their land and proceeded to repeat the same mistakes, so that by the time Jesus came, they were not people of the Word or praise, but people of tradition and a building, which was the Second Temple."

"All this is just too, too good," Harold concluded. And with that, he closed his computer, signaling that the class review had ended and it was time for bed.

★★★★★

The next morning, Harold snuck off to his basement chair for some personal devotional time before the children got up to go to school. He opened his Bible to read from the psalms, and came to rest on Psalm 51:

For the director of music. A psalm of David. When the prophet Nathan came to him after David had committed adultery with Bathsheba.

> *Have mercy on me, O God,*
> *according to your unfailing love;*
> *according to your great compassion*
> *blot out my transgressions.*
> *Wash away all my iniquity*
> *and cleanse me from my sin.*
>
> *For I know my transgressions,*
> *and my sin is always before me.*
> *Against you, you only, have I sinned*
> *and done what is evil in your sight;*
> *so you are right in your verdict*
> *and justified when you judge.*
> *Surely I was sinful at birth,*
> *sinful from the time my mother conceived me.*
> *Yet you desired faithfulness even in the womb;*
> *you taught me wisdom in that secret place.*
>
> *Cleanse me with hyssop, and I will be clean;*
> *wash me, and I will be whiter than snow.*
> *Let me hear joy and gladness;*
> *let the bones you have crushed rejoice.*
> *Hide your face from my sins*

and blot out all my iniquity.

Create in me a pure heart, O God,
and renew a steadfast spirit within me.
Do not cast me from your presence
or take your Holy Spirit from me.
Restore to me the joy of your salvation
and grant me a willing spirit, to sustain me.

Then I will teach transgressors your ways,
so that sinners will turn back to you.
Deliver me from the guilt of bloodshed, O God,
you who are God my Savior,
and my tongue will sing of your righteousness.
Open my lips, Lord,
and my mouth will declare your praise.
You do not delight in sacrifice, or I would bring it;
you do not take pleasure in burnt offerings.
My sacrifice, O God, is a broken spirit;
a broken and contrite heart
you, God, will not despise.

May it please you to prosper Zion,
to build up the walls of Jerusalem.
Then you will delight in the sacrifices of the righteous,
in burnt offerings offered whole;
then bulls will be offered on your altar.

The previous night's class had deeply impacted Harold in many ways and he could not help but apply what he learned to his current church situation. He was on a journey similar to the one the Jews made to Babylon. First, they were in denial as they were relocated to their enemy's homeland in Babylon. They cried out to God to ask how this could have happened. Gradually, however, they realized that they had a role in the events of their day, and they eventually confessed their culpability for the entire affair.

While Harold had not been guilty of adultery or any other moral breach, he saw last night that his heart was not right in the matter of the leadership at the church. He had been arrogant and at times rude, wanting to be right all the time and at any cost. He had not been sensitive to the feelings of the people, naively believing that they needed to change – that they *would* change – as he carried out what he believed to be the will of God for Three Rivers.

Yet, Harold's morning journey into self-awareness and examination went deeper than just his attitude or actions. After last night's class, he realized that he had been so focused on building the church that he had neglected the same things Judah had abandoned as they built their life around the Temple. Harold had based his identity on building a church, and had abandoned his love of the "law" or God's word. Oh, he was still a Bible-believing and Word-preaching Baptist pastor, but he had allowed the work of the church to supplant the two main pillars of their existence: the Word and worship.

Harold faced the fact that he had stopped joining the congregation for worship, instead staying back in his office while the people sang. That was a tradition in many churches, but Harold had felt it was unhealthy, for the people needed to see their shepherd worshiping

God as they were asked to do. Someplace along the line, Harold had stopped joining them and succumbed to the tradition, staying in his office until the singing was finished.

Then there were times when Harold had mixed politics into his messages along with social activism projects. The Lord had convicted him through the class that he had abandoned his first love, which was preaching the word of God to the people of God. This was not about what any other churches or pastors were or were not doing. God was dealing with Harold and he knew it.

He reviewed the message in Psalm 51 again:

Wash away all my iniquity
and cleanse me from my sin.

For I know my transgressions,
and my sin is always before me.
Against you, you only, have I sinned
and done what is evil in your sight;
so you are right in your verdict
and justified when you judge.

"Lord, I've sinned," Harold said out loud. "I've questioned Your faithfulness during this time, but I am the one who has been unfaithful." He read on:

Cleanse me with hyssop, and I will be clean;
wash me, and I will be whiter than snow.
Let me hear joy and gladness;
let the bones you have crushed rejoice.
Hide your face from my sins
and blot out all my iniquity.

"God, I'm not dealing with the deacons or the people, I'm dealing with You." Harold moved out of his chair and on to his knees. He had discovered earlier in his ministry that when he needed a prayer, he could find one in God's word, and today was no exception as he continued to study Psalm 51:

> Create in me a pure heart, O God,
> and renew a steadfast spirit within me.
> Do not cast me from your presence
> or take your Holy Spirit from me.
> Restore to me the joy of your salvation
> and grant me a willing spirit, to sustain me.

> Then I will teach transgressors your ways,
> so that sinners will turn back to you.

"Yes, Lord, create in me a clean heart. Restore to me the joy of my ministry, which is not to build a church, but to proclaim Your kingdom." By now, Harold was weeping but he continued to read:

> Open my lips, Lord,
> and my mouth will declare your praise.
> You do not delight in sacrifice, or I would bring it;
> you do not take pleasure in burnt offerings.
> My sacrifice, O God, is a broken spirit;
> a broken and contrite heart
> you, God, will not despise.

Harold realized then and there that God was trying to break his spirit because he was proud and arrogant. He saw his own sin and when he did, the sins of the people faded from his conscious mind. This was all between him and God, and God was after a broken and contrite heart.

"Lord, forgive me! Lord, help me!" Harold realized that he had some people to see and some business to conduct, but his concern was for how God evaluated his heart and actions, and he recognized that as was said in Daniel 5, "He had been weighed and found deficient." Harold could have tarried longer before the Lord, but he heard the children up and about, and knew in 20 minutes or so he needed to help get breakfast ready and get them off to school. He jotted down some notes in his journal, and then closed the entry by writing, "To be finished at a later date."

CHAPTER 6

On the following Sunday, Harold preached from Psalm 51, and alluded to the fact that God was dealing with him in the areas of pride and arrogance. He knew his enemies were watching and evaluating him, especially in the second service, but he wasn't trying to send them a message as much as acknowledging his journey with God through these difficult days. While he preached, he could not help but notice Hazel Fuller among the people, and he wondered if Sharlene had told her mother they were in class together. It always surprised Harold how he could preach, but then carry on another internal thought process that related to other church matters while he preached.

Harold watched for signs of body language among the crowd, but he saw very little change during his message. Some sat with their arms across their chest, and did not change that during his 22-minute message. Others nodded their heads or uttered a soft amen after he made a point. After both services, he took up his position at the door of the church to greet the people. Some walked by without acknowledging his presence while others shook his hand, pronouncing the perfunctory, "Thank you for the message." There was usually someone who said, "Thanks for the speech," and Harold was always amused when he heard that, for what he had just delivered was anything but a speech.

There were a few people, however, that Harold made a special effort to reach out to, and they were mostly those he knew were not happy with him. He did not believe they would come to see him if he asked them to visit the office, so he determined that he needed to have a face-to-face that morning, and he had rehearsed what he was going to say.

The first person he approached was Deacon Robinson, and Harold said, "Deacon Robinson, may I have a quick word with you?" The Deacon assumed there was some church issue that needed his attention, so he met Pastor Portis in his office.

"Deacon, thank you for seeing me. I just wanted to say that I appreciate your service to the church, and I want to ask your forgiveness for my attitude and behavior over the last year or so. I don't believe I represented the Lord very well, and regardless of what happens next week with the vote, I wanted you to know that I realize I have made some mistakes and I'm sorry," Pastor Portis said, surprising himself with the ease of his delivery.

Deacon Robinson was clearly taken aback by the comments, but he only said, "There's no need to apologize. What's done is done." He was obviously uncomfortable with the topic and gave every indication that he wanted to move on and out of the office.

"Well, I ask you to forgive me, and I'm praying for God's will to be done next week." With that, Deacon Robinson left the office, neither recognizing the request for forgiveness or committing his prayerful attention to the matters at hand.

Pastor Portis then went through the church and tried to do the same with some of the others who he knew were upset with his leadership. As he did, he noticed Deacon Robinson talking with Deacon Washington in the back of the church. It looked like a serious discussion, and as he finished talking with Brother Simpson, a former deacon and head of the trustees, he saw the other two deacons still talking in the rear. He approached them both to see if he could talk with Deacon Washington. When he got near, the men stopped talking and then Deacon Washington said, "Now Pastor Portis, there's no need to try at this late date to affect the vote next week."

Pastor Portis was caught offguard, but pressed through with an explanation. "That's not my intent, Deacon. I just want to make our relationship right despite the events at hand."

Deacon Washington was not buying what Pastor Portis was selling. "No, you're trying to save yourself ahead of the vote to be taken next week. I for one am ready for a transition, and nothing you can say will change my mind."

Pastor Portis was not prepared for the frank comments and had not rehearsed anything to say in response. "Well, that's not the reason for what I'm saying. I only hoped . . ."

The deacons cut him off and informed him, "The meeting next Sunday is at 6 PM. Pastor Amos Windham will be coming to moderate. We'll make our case, then you'll have a chance to respond, and then those present will vote. We'll see you next week." And with that, the deacons left the church.

Harold went back to his office, visibly shaken by the events of the day. Lois had left with the children after the second service since the family had to be at both services due to her role in children's church, so he could not find a friendly face as the last few people filed out of the sanctuary. Harold made his way to his car parked outside the back door. As he was about to get into his car, however, he heard a woman's voice calling him.

"Pastor, may I speak to you for a minute?" the woman inquired.

"Well, yes, would you like to go back into my office?" Pastor Portis responded. It was Hazel Fuller, Sharlene's mother.

"No, this will only take a minute. I wanted to thank you for your message this morning," Hazel began, much to Pastor Portis' surprise. "I think it took a lot of courage to say what you said, and I for one appreciated it very much."

"Why, thank you, Hazel," Harold said, and he meant every word. It was nice to hear a friendly voice.

"I want you to know I'll be present next week, but I'm not sure how I'll vote. I've thought we needed changes in the church, but when they came, I thought they happened too fast," Hazel explained, looking down on the pavement as she talked. "I don't know what to think after today, but I promise I'll be praying for the church and for you and your family this coming week."

Harold wanted to hug her, but did not know if she would think he was trying to win her vote, but he did say, "Hazel, that means a lot to me and us right now. I'll be praying too. Thank you for your honesty."

With that, Harold got in the car and drove off, exclaiming out loud as he got to the first stop sign, "Oh nuts, I forget to mention to Hazel that her daughter and I are classmates." The morning had been quite a jumble of conflicting messages with tension hanging in the air. Harold was glad the vote was next week, but he knew it was going to be a long week ahead. Even so, he was determined to keep up the momentum of his time with the Lord, and he vowed to follow through on whatever the Lord showed him to do.

★★★★★

When Harold got home, Lois inquired about how he felt things went, adding, "I thought you did a good job in your message today." Lois had enough volunteers to cover the children's ministry, so she came upstairs to listen to the sermon.

"Did you?" Harold said with a trace of surprise. "I wasn't sure how it went, to be honest."

"Did you get any other feedback?" Lois asked.

"Well, yes, let's just say I got mixed reviews," Harold said with a smile, "but I don't want to talk about it here or now. Where are the kids? Let's eat!" And with that, Harold went upstairs to wash the ministry off his hands before eating dinner and then going back for the Sunday evening prayer service, before beginning preparations for the week ahead.

★★★★★

Monday arrived too soon for Harold. He opened his eyes and the clock on his nightstand read 4:36. After slipping out of bed, he went downstairs to make coffee, and then proceeded to his spot in the basement family room where he carried out his daily devotions.

Harold tried not to let the comments that were made in church consume him, but he was not doing a good job. He did not give Lois all the gory details of his encounters with the deacons who opposed him, but he knew that she knew more had happened than he had reported. He also knew it was taking its toll on Lois, who was concerned for the family's future. How would they make a living? Where would they be? Would they have to move? Harold and Lois had talked some about those answers, but of course, everything was on hold and up in the air until after the vote, for Harold wanted to keep his trust in God and not assume the worst. That was proving to be difficult after yesterday's church service.

On this morning, Harold turned to Psalm 59, because in one of his textbooks it mentioned this psalm as David's lament over how he was being treated by King Saul:

For the director of music. To the tune of "Do Not Destroy." Of David. A miktam. When Saul had sent men to watch David's house in order to kill him.

Deliver me from my enemies, O God;
be my fortress against those who are attacking me.
Deliver me from evildoers
and save me from those who are after my blood.

See how they lie in wait for me!
Fierce men conspire against me
for no offense or sin of mine, Lord.
I have done no wrong, yet they are ready to attack me.
Arise to help me; look on my plight!
You, Lord God Almighty,
you who are the God of Israel,
rouse yourself to punish all the nations;
show no mercy to wicked traitors.

They return at evening,
snarling like dogs,
and prowl about the city.
See what they spew from their mouths—
the words from their lips are sharp as swords,
and they think, "Who can hear us?"

But you laugh at them, Lord;
you scoff at all those nations.

You are my strength, I watch for you;
you, God, are my fortress,
my God on whom I can rely.

God will go before me
and will let me gloat over those who slander me.
But do not kill them, Lord our shield,
or my people will forget.
In your might uproot them
and bring them down.
For the sins of their mouths,
for the words of their lips,
let them be caught in their pride.
For the curses and lies they utter,
consume them in your wrath,
consume them till they are no more.
Then it will be known to the ends of the earth
that God rules over Jacob.

They return at evening,
snarling like dogs,
and prowl about the city.
They wander about for food
and howl if not satisfied.
But I will sing of your strength,
in the morning I will sing of your love;
for you are my fortress,
my refuge in times of trouble.

You are my strength, I sing praise to you;

> *you, God, are my fortress,*
> *my God on whom I can rely.*

Harold was gaining a greater appreciation for David's writing ability, for he described his suffering and life situation in graphic and colorful terms that stood the test of time. He re-read how David described Saul's men who were outside his house waiting to kill him:

> *They return at evening,*
> *snarling like dogs,*
> *and prowl about the city.*
> *They wander about for food*
> *and howl if not satisfied.*

Harold laughed and said, "ruff, ruff" out loud, for he could actually see the "human" dogs who were Saul's henchmen sniffing around David's abode. *Well,* he thought, *my enemies at the church aren't nearly that bad.* He then turned to read the account of this encounter in 1 Samuel 19:11-17 that produced Psalm 59:

> *Saul sent men to David's house to watch it and to kill him in the morning. But Michal, David's wife, warned him, "If you don't run for your life tonight, tomorrow you'll be killed." So Michal let David down through a window, and he fled and escaped. Then Michal took an idol and laid it on the bed, covering it with a garment and putting some goats' hair at the head. When Saul sent the men to capture David, Michal said, "He is ill." Then Saul sent the men back to see David and told them, "Bring him up to me in his bed so that I may kill him."*

But when the men entered, there was the idol in the bed, and at the head was some goats' hair. Saul said to Michal, "Why did you deceive me like this and send my enemy away so that he escaped?" Michal told him, "He said to me, 'Let me get away. Why should I kill you?'"

There was so much to take in. First, Michal was Saul's daughter, and her father was trying to kill her husband and make her a widow! Then Harold noticed that David escaped his captors, and it caused Harold to think that perhaps he should do the same and simply resign, sparing the church the pain of the coming vote.

Harold was also intrigued by the fact that Michal had to lie to help David escape and, while that worked for the moment, he also realized that later Michal would despise David when he danced before the Lord with all his might. He concluded that Michal was unstable and was no long-term help to David. *Given her father's craziness, what else could you expect?* Harold thought. He also said a prayer of thanksgiving for Lois who, despite her anxiety over their situation, was a spiritual woman who wanted God's will and trusted Him to reveal it without manipulating the circumstances to help it happen. *Lois has been my perfect partner,* Harold thought, and gave thanks to God for her.

Harold also realized that he was not as innocent as David proclaimed himself to be, but still took comfort in the fact that David, the anointed friend of God, was being unjustly persecuted over his leadership role. He saw the same issue at his church. The issue was who was going to lead, the pastor or the deacons: imperfect deacons were persecuting an imperfect pastor over who was anointed or best positioned to lead the church.

Then Harold made a short journey from Psalm 59 back to Psalm 57, which he had studied a week or so ago. This psalm described David's lament over how King Saul, whom he had served and honored, was treating him.

For the director of music. To the tune of "Do Not Destroy." Of David. A miktam.
When he had fled from Saul into the cave.

Have mercy on me, my God, have mercy on me,
for in you I take refuge.
I will take refuge in the shadow of your wings
until the disaster has passed.

I cry out to God Most High,
to God, who vindicates me.
He sends from heaven and saves me,
rebuking those who hotly pursue me—
God sends forth his love and his faithfulness.

I am in the midst of lions;
I am forced to dwell among ravenous beasts—
men whose teeth are spears and arrows,
whose tongues are sharp swords.

Be exalted, O God, above the heavens;
let your glory be over all the earth.

They spread a net for my feet—
I was bowed down in distress.
They dug a pit in my path—

but they have fallen into it themselves.

My heart, O God, is steadfast,
my heart is steadfast;
I will sing and make music.
Awake, my soul!
Awake, harp and lyre!
I will awaken the dawn.

I will praise you, Lord, among the nations;
I will sing of you among the peoples.
For great is your love, reaching to the heavens;
your faithfulness reaches to the skies.

Be exalted, O God, above the heavens;
let your glory be over all the earth.

Harold knew he had to "camp" a little longer at this psalm, for there was even more today that he saw pertaining to his current situation. He took out his journal and determined now to stop writing until he had exhausted his insight:

- This is a prayer as well as a psalm of praise. David praised the Lord even while he agonized over his situation! I need to do the same.

- In this case, David did not take refuge in his wife's deception or help. He put his trust in the Lord and Him alone.

- David's enemies were relentless and powerful! He portrayed them as lions and ravenous beasts with sharp teeth. The sharp teeth seemed to be how they used their mouths to utter words that tore into David's heart and mind.

- These men were not out to hurt David; they wanted to kill him, or at least ruin his future and ability to care for his family. They were ruthless, yet David interspersed his account of their wickedness with praises to God! What's more, he declared that his heart was steadfast. Harold knew how difficult that was to maintain a focus on God when everything else seems to be going wrong, but David did it!

- David did not blame God for his dilemma and did not question God's goodness. He was resolute in his determination to worship God and to give God glory in his situation.

- David was outnumbered but he saw that, with God on his side, he and God constituted a majority.

- David concluded that while he was outnumbered and a fugitive, he had a future because God was going to preserve and protect him. His faith was active and he made plans for the future – "I *will* praise you among the nations."

- David was a spiritual man! In the midst of his own pain and the danger of the day, he saw God's love and faithfulness; he was concerned for God's glory; he determined to sing and make music while his enemies were in hot pursuit; he was committed to give God His due even when things were going against him.

Harold was writing furiously when he heard the family stirring above him. He tried to take his children to school every now and then, and today was one of those days. He made a few more notes because he had an idea for the paper that was due for Thursday's class and he did not want to lose his train of thought. Harold determined that he would start on the paper when he got back from the school run, since he would have the house all to himself. He could hardly wait to get back to write the paper, and was thankful his day had started so early and so well.

★★★★★

Monday went by all too quickly, and it was time to begin what was perhaps Harold's final week at Three Rivers. He decided to make the week as normal as possible, but since word was out in the entire community about the upcoming meeting and vote, most people stayed away from the church office, not scheduling appointments.

The midweek service on Wednesday was sparsely attended, but Harold shared some of the insights he had gained in preparing his paper for class. After service, he greeted people as naturally and normally as possible, but there was a tension in the air that everyone could sense if they were discerning. None of the deacons came to the midweek service, which indicated to Harold that they were united in their purpose of seeing that Harold Portis was no longer the pastor at Three Rivers four days from now.

Harold went to his office before heading home, and he pulled out some index cards he had prepared during his Monday study time. On those cards were some verses from the psalms that he had been studying. He had been reciting them every chance he had, and thought he would read a few verses out loud before he left to lift his spirits and restore his faith and hope:

I sought the Lord, and he answered me;
he delivered me from all my fears.
Those who look to him are radiant;
their faces are never covered with shame.

The angel of the Lord encamps
around those who fear him, and he delivers them"
(Psalm 34:4-5, 7).

The righteous cry out, and the Lord hears them;
he delivers them from all their troubles.
The Lord is close to the brokenhearted
and saves those who are crushed in spirit.

The righteous person may have many troubles,
but the Lord delivers him from them all"
(Psalm 34:17-19).

As a father has compassion on his children,
so the Lord has compassion on those who fear him;

for he knows how we are formed,
he remembers that we are dust" (Psalm 103:13-14).

One of the insights Harold had during this time was that the psalms were not only good to use as vehicles of praise, but they were also wonderful prayers. Therefore, he read and said a few psalm prayers before he left:

Better is one day in your courts
than a thousand elsewhere;
I would rather be a doorkeeper in the house of my God than
dwell in the tents of the wicked.
For the Lord God is a sun and shield;
the Lord bestows favor and honor;
no good thing does he withhold
from those whose walk is blameless.

Lord Almighty, Oblessed is the one who trusts in you"
(Psalm 84:10-12)

When I felt secure, I said,
"I will never be shaken."
Lord, when you favored me,
you made my royal mountain stand firm;
but when you hid your face,
I was dismayed.

To you, Lord, I called;
to the Lord I cried for mercy:
"What is gained if I am silenced,
if I go down to the pit?
Will the dust praise you?
Will it proclaim your faithfulness?

Hear, Lord, and be merciful to me;
Lord, be my help."

You turned my wailing into dancing;
you removed my sackcloth and clothed me with joy,
that my heart may sing your praises and not be silent.
Lord my God, I will praise you forever"
(Psalm 30:6-12).

Feeling buoyant and encouraged, Harold left the church for what he realized could be his last midweek service. He wished he had done some things differently, that he had more time to make things right, to explain himself, and to build relationships, but alas, those ships had probably sailed. For now, Harold had to finish up his work for class the next night, and with that he turned out the light of his office and walked out the side door to his waiting vehicle.

CHAPTER 7

The next morning, Harold was back in his base-ment chair, looking at another psalm, Psalm 116, but this time it was not a psalm of lament or a sad song of woe:

I love the Lord, for he heard my voice;
he heard my cry for mercy.
Because he turned his ear to me,
I will call on him as long as I live.
The cords of death entangled me,
the anguish of the grave came over me;
I was overcome by distress and sorrow.
Then I called on the name of the Lord:

"Lord, save me!"
The Lord is gracious and righteous;
our God is full of compassion.
The Lord protects the unwary;
when I was brought low, he saved me.

Return to your rest, my soul,
for the Lord has been good to you.

For you, Lord, have delivered me from death,
my eyes from tears,
my feet from stumbling,
that I may walk before the Lord
in the land of the living.

I trusted in the Lord when I said,
"I am greatly afflicted";
in my alarm I said,
"Everyone is a liar."

What shall I return to the Lord
for all his goodness to me?

I will lift up the cup of salvation
and call on the name of the Lord.
I will fulfill my vows to the Lord
in the presence of all his people.

Precious in the sight of the Lord
is the death of his faithful servants.
Truly I am your servant, Lord;
I serve you just as my mother did;
you have freed me from my chains.

I will sacrifice a thank offering to you

and call on the name of the Lord.
I will fulfill my vows to the Lord
in the presence of all his people,
in the courts of the house of the Lord—
in your midst, Jerusalem.

Praise the Lord.

This psalm had no heading, so the author is unknown, but the tone of the psalm seemed different than the others Harold had been focusing on because of his church dilemma. This one had hope and was full of vows and commitments from the author of what he would do *when*, not if, the Lord delivered him. Yes, the writer was in some trouble, "Lord, save me," but he had broken through to obtain a confidence that allowed him to command his soul to "return to your rest." Harold had been anything but restful these last few weeks, fretting over his future, how he would support his family, and who in the church was "for" him or "against" him.

Then the phrase "I will lift up the cup of salvation" caught Harold's attention. He immediately thought of Jesus' words as He agonized in the Garden the night of His betrayal:

Going a little farther, he fell with his face to the ground and prayed, "My Father, if it is possible, may this cup be taken from me. Yet not as I will, but as you will." Then he returned to his disciples and found them sleeping. "Couldn't you men keep watch with me for one hour?" he asked Peter. "Watch and pray so that you will not fall into temptation. The spirit is willing, but the flesh is weak." He went away a second time and prayed, "My Father, if it is not possible for this cup to be taken away unless I drink it, may your will be done." When he came back, he again found them sleeping, because their eyes were heavy. So he left them and went away once more and prayed the third time, saying the same thing. Then he returned to the disciples and said to them, "Are you still sleeping and resting? Look, the hour has come, and the Son of Man is delivered into the hands of sinners. Rise! Let us go! Here comes my betrayer!" (Matthew 26:39-46).

Harold saw that for Jesus, the cup of salvation meant that He had to go through something from which He needed "saved," not in a spiritual sense but in a physical one. Jesus lifted up the cup of salvation and drank it, trusting that the Father would make good on His promise found in Psalm 16:

Therefore my heart is glad and my tongue rejoices;
my body also will rest secure,
because you will not abandon me
to the realm of the dead,
nor will you let your faithful one see decay.
You make known to me the path of life;
you will fill me with joy in your presence,
with eternal pleasures at your right hand
(Psalm 16:9-11).

Harold was a Baptist, but what he was seeing was so exhilarating and exciting that he suddenly understood how a Pentecostal could get up and run around the church! Harold's mind was flooded with thoughts of praise and thanksgiving for God's promises of love and protection. Again, he saw the promise of rest, "my body also will rest secure," and He knew God was with him. For Harold, the vote on Sunday didn't matter. What mattered was that God was with him and for that he rejoiced.

Then Harold's mind had another thought. This psalm was part of Book Four, and Harold had learned in his early class studies that the general theme of Book Four for the nation was, "We sinned and the troubles we are in are mostly our fault – but God is good!" When Harold read Psalm 116 in that context, it was clear once again that God was dealing with his heart.

Harold slipped out of his chair and on to his knees: "Lord, I've sinned. I've been arrogant and rude. I've led out of the strength of my own ego, but I was also afraid – of You, of the people, of failure, of what others would think. I ask Your forgiveness, but I also commit to you now that my next leadership opportunity, if you choose to give me one, will be different. No, Lord, *I'll be different.* The psalmist said in Psalm 116:18, *'I will fulfill my vows to the Lord in the presence of all his people, in the courts of the house of the Lord—in your midst, Jerusalem,'* and *I vow to do the same. Teach me how to lead, especially how to lead people, Lord. I need You, but I trust and thank You for this journey, as painful as it's been."*

Harold felt like there was a breakthrough of some kind after he prayed. He did not have any insight into what would happen on Sunday, but that wasn't what he was sensing. He felt a breakthrough in him. Somehow he was different, a changed man when he got up off his knees. Ironically, he had some insight and ideas of how to finish his paper that was due that evening for class, and he moved immediately from his chair to his desk in the corner of the basement and began pulling things together for class. *This is going to be good*, Harold thought, and with that, he began to write his paper on the topic, "Themes that Helped Shape the Book of Psalms."

★★★★★

On Thursday before class, Harold stopped by the church office where Mildred his secretary gave him a few messages but said that things were uneventful around the office. She noted that people had been calling to see what time the Sunday evening vote was, and that a few of the deacons had been having meetings in the church with the financial committee and trustees. Mildred was in an awkward place, but she asked, "How are you and your family doing?"

Harold responded, "We're doing well. Trusting the Lord and praying a lot, but we're okay. Thanks for asking." Harold wondered if he had just lied or not told the whole truth.

Mildred stood and stared, not knowing what to say, "All I can say is that we're praying for you. I've enjoyed working for you." The tone in Mildred's voice sounded like the vote had already been taken and Harold had been removed. Harold wondered if she knew something he didn't.

"Well, it's been mutual, Mildred. If I've done anything to offend you, please forgive me," Harold offered.

"No, you haven't," Mildred answered. "I thought you were doing a good job, but . . ." her voice trailed off and she never finished her thought, and Harold did not ask her to clarify.

"Well, I'm off to class. I guess I'll see you on Sunday," since Mildred took Fridays off.

"Yes, I'll be here," Mildred said, still not quite sure what she should say or how to act, or how much she should share about all she knew of current events at Three Rivers.

★★★★★

Harold pulled up to the seminary and took the usual route to the classroom, where many had already assembled. There was only time for a little small talk before Dr. Jackson came into the room. After fielding prayer requests, Dr. Jackson was about to begin when Sharlene interrupted with a raised hand. "Yes, Ms. Fuller?" Dr. Jackson stopped to ask.

"Before we move on, Dr. Jackson, I think there's another prayer request that's going unspoken tonight," Sharlene explained. "I know our classmate, Pastor Portis, is looking at an important weekend in his church, and I think he would like, or at least he needs, our prayers."

Harold was shocked and glared at her with a I-can't-believe-you-just-did-that look. Before he could respond, Dr. Jackson asked, "Is this true, Pastor?"

"Well, I, er, I don't want to take up class time," Harold fumbled for words before Sharlene interjected once again.

"Pastor Portis is facing a congregational vote this weekend on whether the church wants him to continue as their pastor. My mother's part of the church and has told me all about it," Sharlene explained. "I think he could use our support."

"I see," said Dr. Jackson. "Pastor, may we pray for you?" Without really waiting for a reply, several of the students stood and surrounded Harold, laying their hands on him as Dr. Jackson began to pray. Once Dr. Jackson was done, other students spoke out, asking God to comfort Harold and requesting God to use the circumstances to reveal His love to Harold and his family.

Before Harold knew it, tears were streaming down his cheeks as he listened to the prayers of comfort and peace. He didn't realize how much emotion he was carrying over the ordeal, and he did not know whether to be embarrassed or relieved. It didn't matter, however, for the tears kept on coming.

When the time of prayer finished, all Harold could say was "thank you," but the focus on him and his situation was far from over. This night would be a night that Harold would always remember, for it was a night when he would come face-to-face with his life purpose, and he would never be the same from this point forward.

★★★★★

Dr. Jackson was the first one to speak after the

time of prayer. "Thank you, Ms. Fuller, for bringing this to our attention. We'd be remiss if we didn't stand with our brother in his hour of need. Pastor, is there anything you'd like to say?"

Harold was hesitant, for he did not want to paint anyone at his church in a bad light. He also didn't know if anyone in class knew someone at his church and whether what he said would get back to his church members.

Dr. Jackson anticipated his concerns and said to the class, "I expect what we discuss in these next moments will stay in this classroom and not go outside. If you can't make that commitment, I urge you to take a coffee break and we'll come get you when this discussion is finished." No one moved, and so Dr. Jackson motioned for Harold to speak.

"This class has been a tremendous blessing," Harold began, "coming at just the right time. I've learned so much and it's been incredibly helpful in this season. My wife's waiting for me to come home tonight to share with her what I've learned from all of you and from my own studies. It's all been a lifesaver."

Harold went on to share what he had been learning about himself and about his style of leadership. "I've made many mistakes, and I've tried to seek out those who I know I offended to ask their forgiveness. The problem is that now it looks like I'm doing that to sway or influence their vote. It's awkward."

Dr. Jackson interrupted to say, "There's never a bad time to do the right thing. Go on. I want us all to listen to this, because if you're going to make ministry your life's work, you'll encounter a situation like this eventually. Let's see what we can learn from our pastor brother."

"If I may, Doctor, I would like to share a little from my paper," Harold asked, and Dr. Jackson nodded approval. With that nod, Harold stood and moved to the front of the room where he could use the board if he felt so led. Dr. Jackson surprised everyone by taking Harold's seat, like he was the student and Harold suddenly appointed to be the teacher.

★★★★★

Harold began, "Tonight we were to turn in our paper on a theme or themes that helped shape the content in the psalms. I chose as my topic the role that King Saul played in their development." Some of the students took out their iPads and notebooks to take some notes, and Harold felt empowered by the fact that they were that "into" what he was going to say.

"When you go through what I'm going through, hurtful things take place in the church, the place you least expect them to occur," Harold explained. "I've acknowledged to God that I made mistakes and I know I must take ownership and learn from them. But now I'm being pursued, if that's the right word, by those who feel like they own the church, who don't want any change to come about, and they have seized my mistakes as a reason to oppose the changes."

"As I studied the psalms, I noticed how many of David's psalms were affected and even inspired by the persecution he experienced from his father-in-law, King Saul. Specifically, I noted the headings in Psalms 9, 11, 17, 31, 34, 35, 52, 56, 57, 59, 63, 64, and 142 were all related to what happened in David's life because of Saul's mistreatment. We can safely say that the psalms were seasoned by Saul's role in David's life, even though Saul's name was never mentioned, except in the headings."

Dr. Jackson interrupted, "It's interesting how the headings contribute to the impact the psalms have. Did you pay much attention to them before this class?"

Harold shook his head and said, "I absolutely did not, but I do now!"

"Keep in mind that we believe the headings were added at some point much later after the psalms were compiled. We don't believe they are part of inspired Scripture, but we believe they are reliable guides. Go on," Dr. Jackson said, "I'll try not to interrupt again."

"No, I welcome your insight and input, as well as that of the class."

"Then I have a question," said one of Harold's classmates. "Do you think David wrote those psalms while he was going through what he was, or after the fact?"

Harold did not hesitate. "I believe it was during, which is an amazing thing. You've all prayed for me, which I appreciate, because of what I'm encountering at my church. It's been a difficult time and the last thing I wanted to think about doing was writing. In fact, if it wasn't for this class, I would probably be hiding out in my basement office, waiting for the axe to fall."

"I believe the Lord has showed me that I'm to write more, just like David did, drawing on my experiences to help teach others. I think as a pastor I've been trying to portray myself as being who I thought God wanted me to be, who I thought the people wanted me to be," Harold said, in full teaching mode, "instead of who I truly was."

"You're a good teacher," someone in the class proclaimed.

And it was then that Harold had an epiphany, an enlightening moment that would change his life. Once again, he noticed his ability to be speaking but having an internal conversation about something else. This something else was worth remembering, so he took a breath, made a note so he would not forget the insight he just had, and then continued with the lesson. Little did he realize that what he wrote on that paper would be the most precious possession of his ordeal at Three Rivers Baptist.

★★★★★

Harold could not wait to get home and Lois could not wait for him to come home. There had not been many things to look forward to in those final weeks of summer, but the after-class debriefings were one of them. Lois had an apple pie ready and waiting for Harold as he walked up from the garage, and she herself was set up in her mini-kitchen classroom, ready to hear about the evening's class.

"How was it?" she asked, as Harold put his

briefcase down in the living room.

"Fantastic! What a night! I ended up teaching almost the entire class! Dr. Jackson took my seat and I shared the content of this week's paper, and it took on a life of its own," Harold enthused. "After I finished, I fielded questions and things just wouldn't stop. We never even took a class break, with people running out to the restroom and hurrying back so they wouldn't miss anything that was going on or being said!"

Lois was glad to hear that, for her husband who had to bear the brunt of the recall vote that was now only a few days away, had not had much to celebrate in ministry lately.

"Oh yeah," Harold added, "the class prayed for me before class began. They all gathered around and prayed some really encouraging things. Sharlene, Hazel's daughter, brought it up and said she thought they should pray for me. I suppose her mother filled her in on some of what's going on at the church."

"Then Dr. Jackson shared at one point how the same thing had happened to him many years ago when he was a young pastor. He said as painful as it was, it was the best thing that ever happened to him, for it set him on a course that was more purposeful and fulfilling. He and his family went on the missions field in Asia and when he returned to the U.S., he took a teaching position in Virginia and then here in Pittsburgh," Harold explained. "He and I talked for quite a while after class, but I told him I had another class to go to here at home, and he laughed and dismissed me."

"So what happened that you took over Dr. Jackson's class?" Lois wanted to know.

"We had to write a paper on a theme that helped shape the book of Psalms and my paper was on the relationship between Saul and David, and how many of the individual psalms came out of Saul's treatment of David," Harold said, as he went to retrieve a copy of his paper from his briefcase to use as a guide.

Lois took up her position at the kitchen table, ready to learn, and Harold, even though he had taught earlier in the evening, was ready to instruct.

"Ok, Lois, as best I can tell, these are the psalms David wrote whose headings or content indicate they had something to do with how Saul treated him. Now basically, if Saul doesn't treat David as he did, does David touch the depths of his pain and write material that still inspires and edifies us today? Probably not! Therefore, God used Saul's persecution to develop David's ability to find, understand, and then communicate to others the ways of God. Romans 8:28 was already at work in David's life: 'And we know that in all things God works for the good of those who love him, who have been called according to his purpose.' And he lived 1,100 years before it was written."

"What's more, when I read the psalms and read about the historical setting that produced that psalm, it creates a more meaningful, relevant Bible study," Harold added.

Lois, ever the good student, asked, "Can you give me an example?"

"Certainly," Harold said as he had a fork full of Lois' apple pie. "Let's consider Psalm 142 where the heading says, "A *maskil* of David. When he was in the cave. A prayer."

"What's a maskil?" Lois interrupted.

"We aren't exactly sure," Harold responded. "It may have been a special musical interpretation or some believe it simply represented a psalm with a special message presented in a creative way."

"Thank you," Lois said in her best school-girl voice.

"You're welcome," Harold said in a deep, authoritative voice. "Now don't interrupt again. Let's read Psalm 142."

> *I cry aloud to the Lord;*
> *I lift up my voice to the Lord for mercy.*
> *I pour out before him my complaint;*
> *before him I tell my trouble.*
>
> *When my spirit grows faint within me,*
> *it is you who watch over my way.*
> *In the path where I walk*
> *people have hidden a snare for me.*
> *Look and see, there is no one at my right hand;*
> *no one is concerned for me.*
> *I have no refuge;*
> *no one cares for my life.*
>
> *I cry to you, Lord;*
> *I say, "You are my refuge,*
> *my portion in the land of the living."*

Listen to my cry,
for I am in desperate need;
rescue me from those who pursue me,
for they are too strong for me.
Set me free from my prison,
that I may praise your name.
Then the righteous will gather about me
because of your goodness to me.

"Now let's consider the story of when David was in the cave to see what we can learn from the psalm and its historical setting in 1 Samuel 22:1-5," Harold continued.

David left Gath and escaped to the cave of Adullam. When his brothers and his father's household heard about it, they went down to him there. All those who were in distress or in debt or discontented gathered around him, and he became their commander. About four hundred men were with him. From there David went to Mizpah in Moab and said to the king of Moab, "Would you let my father and mother come and stay with you until I learn what God will do for me?" So he left them with the king of Moab, and they stayed with him as long as David was in the stronghold. But the prophet Gad said to David, "Do not stay in the stronghold. Go into the land of Judah." So David left and went to the forest of Hereth.

"There's so much there, Lois, and it's so pertinent to what we're going through," Harold proclaimed with excitement. They both went into a long discussion of what the psalm and the story meant to them at this point in their lives, and Lois created a summary of their dialogue:

1. David took time out in the cave from his distress to pray and seek the Lord.

2. David never blamed God for his troubles.

3. David was alone in his troubles (they were unique to his purpose and calling), but not truly alone, for God was with him.

4. David was imprisoned by his circumstances as he prayed that God would free him, yet he was freer than Saul who was bound by fear and anger.

5. It is obvious from 1 Samuel 22 that God did free David from the confines of his cave to do what he had to do.

6. David was concerned for his family and made provision for their protection while he went about his business.

7. David had a group accompanying him that was also in serious trouble, just like he was. He could not retreat or isolate himself. He had to be a leader!

8. The spiritual forces aligned against David were real and were out to destroy him, not just hinder or hurt him.

9. David took time to be creative even when

faced with danger and when he could have excused himself from creating.

10. David's prayer and praise were determined by and shaped, in part, by the persecution of Saul. Therefore, God will perfect our praise and deepen our prayer life through the trials and tribulations of following Him!

Then Harold went on to share his insight into suffering that he had gleaned from the New Testament. "You know, Lois, there's an aspect of suffering that produces something in us that nothing else can. As I reflected on Jesus' betrayal and time in the Garden when He sweat blood, I was led to two passages:

> *During the days of Jesus' life on earth, he offered up prayers and petitions with fervent cries and tears to the one who could save him from death, and he was heard because of his reverent submission. Son though he was, he learned obedience from what he suffered and, once made perfect, he became the source of eternal salvation for all who obey him and was designated by God to be high priest in the order of Melchizedek (Hebrews 5:7-10).*

> *Therefore, since Christ suffered in his body, arm yourselves also with the same attitude, because whoever suffers in the body is done with sin. As a result, they do not live the rest of their earthly lives for evil human desires, but rather for the will of God (1 Peter 4:1-2).*

"Jesus suffered, Lois, but it perfected His humanity, and made Him more well-rounded and mature, and suffering does the same for us. If I hadn't gone through this time at Three Rivers, I'd never have had the insight I found in the psalms, never known God's goodness as I have now," and as Harold spoke, the tears began to flow as they did in class. Of course, Lois joined him in a tearful duet.

"I've concluded that those who oppose us at Three Rivers did us a favor for which I will be forever grateful," Harold concluded. "They were our enemies, but they have turned out to be our friends!" After they talked, shared, and took more notes, Harold and Lois took time to pray together and recited Psalm 142 in unison. By then it was around midnight, and Harold debated whether or not to share the epiphany he had received and written down during class. It was late and Lois already had so much weighing on her mind, so he decided not to share it until they both were better rested, for it was going to be quite a shock to her – just as it had been to him.

★★★★★

The next morning, Harold assumed his position in his basement lounge chair for his personal devotions. As soon as he awakened, he was thinking about Psalm 139 in the context of what he had seen in class the previous evening. He turned there to read it in its entirety:

You have searched me, Lord,
and you know me.

You know when I sit and when I rise;
you perceive my thoughts from afar.
You discern my going out and my lying down;
you are familiar with all my ways.
Before a word is on my tongue
you, Lord, know it completely.
You hem me in behind and before,
and you lay your hand upon me.
Such knowledge is too wonderful for me,
too lofty for me to attain.

Where can I go from your Spirit?
Where can I flee from your presence?
If I go up to the heavens, you are there;
if I make my bed in the depths, you are there.
If I rise on the wings of the dawn,
if I settle on the far side of the sea,
even there your hand will guide me,
your right hand will hold me fast.
If I say, "Surely the darkness will hide me
and the light become night around me,"
even the darkness will not be dark to you;
the night will shine like the day,
for darkness is as light to you.

For you created my inmost being;
you knit me together in my mother's womb.
I praise you because I am
fearfully and wonderfully made;
your works are wonderful,
I know that full well.
My frame was not hidden from you

when I was made in the secret place,
when I was woven together in the depths of the earth.
Your eyes saw my unformed body;
all the days ordained for me were written in your book
before one of them came to be.
How precious to me are your thoughts, God!
How vast is the sum of them!
Were I to count them,
they would outnumber the grains of sand—
when I awake, I am still with you.

If only you, God, would slay the wicked!
Away from me, you who are bloodthirsty!
They speak of you with evil intent;
your adversaries misuse your name.
Do I not hate those who hate you, Lord,
and abhor those who are in rebellion against you?
I have nothing but hatred for them;
I count them my enemies.
Search me, God, and know my heart;
test me and know my anxious thoughts.
See if there is any offensive way in me,
and lead me in the way everlasting.

This was another psalm David had written, but the context for this oft-quoted psalm caught Harold's attention. Most people look at or quote verse 14: "I praise you for I am fearfully and wonderfully made." Harold was now looking at what was going on in David's life that caused him to pen those comforting words.

David had been a fugitive, fleeing the murderous intent of King Saul. As he fled, he concluded that he could not flee from or outrun God. God was with David wherever he went, and David was amazed, for God was with him because of who he was, not despite who he was. God knew David's thoughts before he thought them, his words before he uttered them, and God was faithful to remain. While David was searching for hiding places to shield himself and his followers from Saul's army, David was always in God's full view – even David's imperfections!

Even though David's life was in danger, he took time to meditate on God's goodness, who God is, and what He does for David. Then Harold saw a line he had never noticed before in verse 18. David declared that when he awakens every morning, he is still with God. David was amazed that God put up with him even though David was less than perfect and incapable of grasping God's thoughts and the magnitude and importance of God's presence.

Then David prayed to the Lord: "Oh God, I wish you would wipe out my enemies." But David was not selfishly trying to rid the earth of those who made his life miserable. David hated his enemies because they hated God and were in rebellion against God's choice for king. David was an enemy to his enemies because they were enemies of God. It wasn't about David; it was about God.

Harold slipped out of his chair to his knees: "Lord, I have made this vote and my role here at Three Rivers about me, when it's really about You! Forgive me, Lord!" Then Harold prayed the last verses of Psalm 139:

Search me, God, and know my heart;
test me and know my anxious thoughts.
See if there is any offensive way in me,
and lead me in the way everlasting.

Harold was sure he had never prayed those verses as he just had. He wanted God to show him who he was and is, yet the backdrop for that request was not fear but the truth that Harold was "fearfully and wonderfully made." "God, you are intimately acquainted with all my ways," Harold prayed, "and you still love me! You made me who I am. You made me serious, aggressive, zealous, open to change. That's who I am! You don't want me to change that but to use it for your purpose to fulfill my purpose, the purpose You have given me!" Having said that, Harold began crying yet again, and was glad, as he realized he needed to be softer and more broken before the Lord and with people, and God was using his current situation to create that condition in his life and heart.

This line of prayer caused Harold to turn to Psalm 56, another psalm of David penned when he was under distress due to Saul:

For the director of music. To the tune of "A Dove
on Distant Oaks." Of David. A miktam. When the
Philistines had seized him in Gath.

Be merciful to me, my God,
for my enemies are in hot pursuit;
all day long they press their attack.
My adversaries pursue me all day long;
in their pride many are attacking me.

When I am afraid, I put my trust in you.
In God, whose word I praise—
in God I trust and am not afraid.
What can mere mortals do to me?

All day long they twist my words;
all their schemes are for my ruin.
They conspire, they lurk,
they watch my steps,
hoping to take my life.
Because of their wickedness do not let them escape;
in your anger, God, bring the nations down.

Record my misery;
list my tears on your scroll—
are they not in your record?
Then my enemies will turn back
when I call for help.
By this I will know that God is for me.

In God, whose word I praise,
in the Lord, whose word I praise—
in God I trust and am not afraid.
What can man do to me?

I am under vows to you, my God;
I will present my thank offerings to you.
For you have delivered me from death
and my feet from stumbling,
that I may walk before God
in the light of life.

Harold researched the story mentioned in the psalm's

title and that took him to 1 Samuel 21:10-15:

> *That day David fled from Saul and went to Achish king of Gath. But the servants of Achish said to him, "Isn't this David, the king of the land? Isn't he the one they sing about in their dances: "'Saul has slain his thousands, and David his tens of thousands'?" David took these words to heart and was very much afraid of Achish king of Gath. So he pretended to be insane in their presence; and while he was in their hands he acted like a madman, making marks on the doors of the gate and letting saliva run down his beard. Achish said to his servants, "Look at the man! He is insane! Why bring him to me? Am I so short of madmen that you have to bring this fellow here to carry on like this in front of me? Must this man come into my house?"*

Harold laughed out loud when he read what David did to escape the clutches of Achish, king of Gath, but Harold saw that David was no longer fleeing his enemies. In this case, he had been captured by his enemies. It was then that David resorted to acting the fool so he could escape. Harold had never noticed that David had been captured, yet David was still writing, still praising, still praying as evidenced by Psalm 56.

Harold had turned to that psalm because he was thinking of verse eight that addressed the topic of David's tears in light of Harold's brokenness: "Record my misery; list my tears on your scroll—are they not in your record?" In this case, Harold turned to the King James Version to read the request that David made in his anguish: "Thou tellest my wanderings: put thou my tears into thy bottle: are they not in thy book?"

Harold cried out, "Oh God, don't let this suffering of mine go to waste. Keep track of my tears, Lord. Put them in a bottle so we can both refer to them later when all this is over. Don't let all this go for naught!"

Harold reached for his journal and began to record his thoughts and impressions of what the Lord was revealing to him about his future. He wrote furiously and was surprised by what he was hearing and seeing. *God really was with me, not despite who I am but because of who I am!* Harold wrote, which only caused him to bury his face in the seat of his chair as he knelt before it. For the next 25 minutes, Harold prayed, and then wrote; wrote and then prayed; prayed and then re-read Psalm 56 and Psalm 139 – and wrote some more.

Before he finished, he took out the paper that contained the words he had jotted down during class. "Lord, thank You for this insight into who I am. Thank You for showing me my future." Harold felt the tears coming again, but he heard stirrings upstairs, telling him it was time to get on with life and chauffeur his kids to school.

Harold took one last look at his journal entries and was more convinced than ever before that he had found his purpose through this ordeal, and he was not going to waste his tears. He was going to put them in a bottle, so to speak, so he could keep them as part of his journey and pilgrimage with the Lord, of which this church dilemma was an important part.

CHAPTER 8

After Harold dropped his children off at school, he decided to go into the office, which he seldom did on Friday unless he had a counseling appointment. When he pulled up to the church, he saw more cars there than usual and wondered what was up. It was also strange to see Mildred's car there, because she usually took Friday off. He assumed it was a meeting of a committee, but it was still unusual for that to take place on a weekday during work hours.

As Harold accessed his office through the side door, he walked in on a meeting. It was obvious from the looks on everyone's faces that they did not expect him, just like he did not expect to see them. There in his office were five of the deacons, and all stopped talking when he walked in.

"Pastor, good morning," one of the deacons said without looking at him. "We needed to have a private meeting and thought we could use your office since you are seldom here on Friday. We will move," and with that, everyone started to gather up some papers to move out.

"No, no that's fine," Harold said, trying to be non-chalant about the awkward confrontation. "I just stopped in for a minute to pick up some files. By the way, is everything all set for Sunday's meeting."

Another deacon responded, "Uh, why, yes it is. Six o'clock. We were just going over the meeting agenda."

At that point, Mildred came in and announced, "Brothers, Pastor Marshall is on the line," and then stopped as she saw Pastor Portis. She had not heard Harold come in and looked flustered and embarrassed for the few seconds she was there before she went back to her office.

Then Harold understood a bit more about what was going on. Pastor Marshall was the moderator for the Sunday night meeting, and the deacons were obviously talking to him to outline their concerns or hopes for the meeting, Harold wasn't sure which. At the same time, Harold finally realized that there had been a leak in his office to the deacons, and that leak or link had been Mildred.

Deacon Robinson instructed Mildred, "Please tell Pastor Marshall that something has come up and we will talk to him later," but he was not sure she had heard him because she exited the office so quickly. "Brothers, I believe we should take our business elsewhere," and with that, everyone got up to leave.

As they left, they forgot to take a folder that was sitting on one of the empty chairs at the conference table. Harold almost called out for them to retrieve it, but for some reason, he decided to open it and examine the contents.

In the folder was a print out of all the names with phone numbers and emails for the Three Rivers membership list. There were brackets around groups of names with the name of a deacon outside the bracket, and Harold knew that the deacons had divided up the list to contact the membership before Sunday's meeting. He knew they were not calling the members to ask for their support to keep him as Three River's pastor.

He also found a copy of the anonymous letter he had found slipped under his door a few Sundays ago. That letter had a sticky note on it, which read: "As we discussed, this was written and delivered – M." Harold realized the M stood for Mildred; she had written the letter!

Harold was trembling, and a few scenarios ran through his mind. He thought of running out and throwing the folder at the deacons who were still present. He considered calling Mildred in and confronting her with the list and note, for he knew she would have been the one to print out the list for the deacons to use. Harold also thought of getting in his car, driving home, and never coming back.

But then Harold harkened back to his devotional time and thought, *This is what David felt – the betrayal, people moving behind his back, being pursued by those who wanted to mar what he did and destroy who he was.* Harold left the folder on the chair where he had found it, and without saying good bye, left through the same side door he had entered. When he got into his car, he retrieved his Bible and journal, which he had put in the back seat instead of leaving it at home for some unknown reason. Now he understood why it was close by.

Since Harold was speechless and did not know what to say, he decided to pray Psalm 17, which he had glanced at during his morning devotions, but did not have time to probe:

A prayer of David.

Hear me, Lord, my plea is just;
listen to my cry.
Hear my prayer—
it does not rise from deceitful lips.
Let my vindication come from you;
may your eyes see what is right.

Though you probe my heart,
though you examine me at night and test me,
you will find that I have planned no evil;
my mouth has not transgressed.
Though people tried to bribe me,
I have kept myself from the ways of the violent
through what your lips have commanded.

My steps have held to your paths;
my feet have not stumbled.

I call on you, my God, for you will answer me;
turn your ear to me and hear my prayer.
Show me the wonders of your great love,
you who save by your right hand
those who take refuge in you from their foes.
Keep me as the apple of your eye;
hide me in the shadow of your wings
from the wicked who are out to destroy me,
from my mortal enemies who surround me.

They close up their callous hearts,
and their mouths speak with arrogance.
They have tracked me down, they now surround me,
with eyes alert, to throw me to the ground.
They are like a lion hungry for prey,
like a fierce lion crouching in cover.

Rise up, Lord, confront them, bring them down;
with your sword rescue me from the wicked.
By your hand save me from such people, Lord,
from those of this world whose reward is in this life.
May what you have stored up
for the wicked fill their bellies;
may their children gorge themselves on it,
and may there be leftovers for their little ones.
As for me, I will be vindicated and will see your face;
when I awake, I will be satisfied
with seeing your likeness.

Harold could not help but shed tears as he prayed

and he was hoping someone, anyone would come out that back door, see him, and feel remorse for the pain they had caused him. He fantasized that they would ask his forgiveness for what they had put him and his family through, and pray for him, calling off the vote meeting at this late hour. But alas, no one appeared, no one showed up, and no one probably cared.

It was time for Harold to go home and wait for Lois to come home from school so they could talk. Then he had to prepare for what he felt like would be the longest weekend of his life. He considered trying to find someone at the last minute to fill Sunday's pulpit but he had a message, and he was going to deliver it, even if he had to do so to an empty church. First, however, he and his wife had to be on the same page where their future was concerned, and they had to talk before the kids came home. Harold took the paper with the insight from class about his future and placed it on the front seat next to him so he could look at it on drive home. He could hardly wait for Lois to get home after school.

★★★★★

On Saturday, Harold received a call from one of the deacons making sure he knew about the time for the Sunday meeting. *This is probably the fourth time they have reminded me of the time,* Harold thought. This deacon had not been at the church the day before, so he did not know that Harold had walked in on the deacons meeting. Then the deacon added something totally unexpected, "Pastor, I would suggest that your wife not be present at the meeting tomorrow night. It may not be a pleasant meeting."

Harold was stunned by the suggestion, but he heard himself respond, "My wife will be there, but thank you for your concern." When Harold told Lois about the call, her anger was visible and quick. "You tell that deacon that I'll be there and if he or anyone tries to stop me, I'm going to whip . . ."

But before she could finish, Harold raised his hand and Lois finished by saying, "him up a nice sweet potato pie!" They looked at each other and laughed, both wondering how they could laugh at a time like this. They were committed to see this ordeal through to the end as a team, so they took a moment to pray, away from the children, who knew about the meeting, but not about the implications of what may take place.

"Speaking of sweet potato pie," Harold said, "is there any left of the one you made the other day?" Harold was upset, but he still had his appetite, and there was no use letting good sweet potato pie go to waste over a few disgruntled deacons.

★★★★★

Harold was surprised by how good he felt when he got up on Sunday morning. He had his message ready and things felt like a normal Sunday, until he arrived at church. He always got there early, around 7:30, to go over his message one more time. The music team was there getting ready to rehearse, but everyone was on edge and distant. Having never been through anything like this, Harold thought maybe it was just him. As the morning wore on into the second service, however, he noticed attendance was down and people were less ready to greet him – and one another for that matter.

Harold suddenly regretted that he did not have a guest minister come in to speak, and he wondered if he even had the right message to share. It was a basic message on forgiveness, and he wondered if people would think he was talking to them about forgiving him, or talking to himself about forgiving them – of if they would hear anything he said at all. He briefly considered going home with the excuse that he was ill, which would not have been very far from the truth.

Harold prayed and then he decided to go about his business like it was a normal Sunday. He greeted people, sat in on a Sunday School class or two, and tried hard not to evaluate if those he was greeting were for or against his continued service.

Before he knew it, it was 10:30 and time to begin the second service with Lois present in the front row, having taken another break from children's church to be present. As Harold watched the service unfold, one thing became clear to him: The church would continue with or without him, as it had done for many decades. He realized that church people knew how to "do" church, and it would be done as it had always been done with or without his presence.

The key issue for Harold was that God had something for him to do, a purpose, and he was seeing that more clearly than ever before. He looked at Lois, and she reached over and squeezed his hand, mouthing the words, "I love you." With that, Harold had to smile and thought to himself, "My most important congregation is next to me with two more downstairs in youth church. If they are for me, then I'll be okay."

And with that, Harold took his position in the pulpit after the offerings to deliver the Sunday message, probably for the last time at Three Rivers Baptist Church.

★★★★★

When Harold got home after church, he asked Lois how she felt it went.

"I thought you did a great job," Lois said with a huge smile accompanied by a big hug. "But I think our kids could use a pep talk," Lois added.

With that suggestion, Harold went upstairs to visit his two children. "Hi guys," he said as he knocked on the door of Sharon's room, where her brother was also sitting. "How's things? How did church go?"

"It was awful," Sharon said and began to cry. Nathan nodded his head in agreement. "One of the kids said that there was no way you were going to win the vote tonight, and you'll be out of a job. We're going to have to move and I'll lose all my friends," Sharon said as she buried her face in the comforter on her bed.

"Hey, hey," Harold said as he sat down on the edge of the bed. "That vote tonight is in God's hands, but it's time we told you what your mother and I have decided is the right course for us to take." And with that

Harold pulled out the paper he had written on while he was making his class presentation. He shared what that meant and what he was going to say at the meeting so that his kids would know ahead of everyone else. When they heard, it seemed to calm them both, for which Harold was relieved. *If it could only have the same effect on me*, Harold thought, as he invited the children to join them downstairs for their Sunday meal, after which they would watch the Steelers preseason game before Harold had to go back to church

★★★★★

Harold and Lois went to the church together for the Sunday evening service, which was unusual, for they often drove separately. It felt like they were going as visitors to their own church, for they had no role in the evening's agenda. Pastor Marshall would be there to moderate, and the deacons would make their "case" of why they felt Harold should no longer continue as the pastor. Then Harold would present his side of the story, and then the congregation would vote. It would be a simple majority to either remove Harold or retain him As they drove, Lois read Psalm 16 in its entirety:

A miktam of David.

Keep me safe, my God,
for in you I take refuge.

I say to the Lord, "You are my Lord;
apart from you I have no good thing."
I say of the holy people who are in the land,
"They are the noble ones in whom is all my delight."

*Those who run after other gods will
suffer more and more.
I will not pour out libations of blood to such gods
or take up their names on my lips.*

*Lord, you alone are my portion and my cup;
you make my lot secure.
The boundary lines have fallen
for me in pleasant places;
surely I have a delightful inheritance.
I will praise the Lord, who counsels me;
even at night my heart instructs me.
I keep my eyes always on the Lord.
With him at my right hand, I will not be shaken.*

*Therefore my heart is glad and my tongue rejoices;
my body also will rest secure,
because you will not abandon me
to the realm of the dead,
nor will you let your faithful one see decay.
You make known to me the path of life;
you will fill me with joy in your presence,
with eternal pleasures at your right hand.*

Then Harold asked her to turn to Psalm 43 and read
that as well:

*Vindicate me, my God,
and plead my cause
against an unfaithful nation.
Rescue me from those who are
deceitful and wicked.
You are God my stronghold.*

Why have you rejected me?
Why must I go about mourning,
oppressed by the enemy?
Send me your light and your faithful care,
let them lead me;
let them bring me to your holy mountain,
to the place where you dwell.
Then I will go to the altar of God,
to God, my joy and my delight.
I will praise you with the lyre,
O God, my God.

Why, my soul, are you downcast?
Why so disturbed within me?
Put your hope in God,
for I will yet praise him,
my Savior and my God.

Harold laughed to himself when he thought of the message in Psalm 43. Being vindicated in the meeting that evening was more than he could hope for, but he hoped in the long run that his leadership and efforts on behalf of the church would be recognized. He knew the recognition would have to come from the Lord though.

"Thank God for the psalms," Harold declared, and Lois agreed. Those declarations of pain, hope, and honesty amidst life's struggles had taken on a whole new meaning for them both through this ordeal. Harold entered the church, not through the side door to his office, but through the front door like everyone else. He shook some hands, thanked people for coming (which he felt was rather odd, sort of like thanking someone for attending his execution), and then took his usual seat in the front right of the church with Lois at his side.

Deacon Robinson called the meeting to order and opened in prayer, after which he introduced Pastor Marshall, who would preside over the meeting. Pastor Marshall, who was sitting on the platform, took the microphone, welcomed everybody and said that the meeting would be conducted in the spirit of brotherly love and kindness. He said that what was at stake was the will of God for Three Rivers and for Pastor Portis, and he would not tolerate any inappropriate debate or derogatory comments.

Harold had promised he was not going to turn around to see who was present, but he broke his vow and looked over his shoulder, more to see how many were present and not who. As he glanced around, he estimated that there 150 people present, and then he made eye contact with a surprise visitor. It was Sharlene from class sitting with Hazel, her mother. Sharlene smiled and put her hands together in a way to say that she was praying for Harold. She also pointed to her right, and there Harold saw a few more students from his Thursday night class who had come, obviously for moral support. He returned the smile to Sharlene, waved at his fellow students, and then refocused his attention on the proceedings. As he did, he pulled out the statement he was prepared to read when it was his time to speak.

Last Thursday in class, Harold had been confronted with how much he loved teaching in front of that class. He had a vision of him doing what Dr. Jackson was doing in a seminary setting somewhere, and one (or maybe more) of his books being used as the textbooks. Harold accepted that night that he was a teacher and he had made up his mind to pursue that course of action, which would require him to obtain his doctorate. He looked at the paper he had written during his lecture and he realized what he had was his purpose statement:

My purpose is to equip God's soldiers in
the field with truth from His word.

When he discussed it with Lois, she was surprised, for being a pastor was all he and they had ever considered, but it made sense to her. She had agreed to continue working as a teacher so Harold could continue his schooling full time. The statement he had prepared was the announcement of his resignation before the church had the chance to vote him out. He read over the statement, missing some of what Pastor Marshall had to say:

*It was great sadness but also with a sense of excitement for the future that I announce tonight that there will be no need for a congregational vote. After prayerful consideration and discussion with my family, I hereby announce my resignation as pastor of Three Rivers Baptist Church. I want to thank all of you for your love and commitment to me and my family during my five years as your pastor. It has not been dull and I know that I have made some mistakes, **many mistakes**, and some of them have led us to this night's proceedings. This morning I spoke on forgiveness, and if I have offended anyone,*

I humbly ask your forgiveness and would be happy to meet with you one-on-one to be more specific about my wrongs and my need for forgiveness.

My plans are to continue my education and pursue a teaching position with a seminary or university to express my gift of teaching and ministry. I apologize that it took this long for me to make this decision, for I truly wanted God's will to be revealed through our vote this evening, but it has become clear to me that my lack of support here at Three Rivers will make the way forward difficult. I believe the church deserves leadership in whom it has confidence so that the wonderful legacy and ministry of Three Rivers Baptist may continue. On behalf of my family, I want to thank you all for your love, support, and commitment to the Lord during our five years here. May God bless you, and please pray for my family and me if the Lord brings us to mind.

"I will now ask that the Deacon Robinson come and present the leadership's perspective on the current state of Three Rivers Baptist Church," and after he said Pastor Marshall sat in the pastor's chair on the platform while Deacon Robinson took the microphone.

Deacon Robinson welcomed everyone and then began to report on what he and the deacons considered to be the declining situation at Three Rivers. He went over the decisions that he and the deacons felt were detrimental to the spiritual health and future of the congregation that led the deacons to call for the special Sunday night meeting. It was not pleasant for Harold and Lois to sit through what amounted to an indictment against their ministry time at Three Rivers, but they listened with as much composure as anyone could be expected to have. After Deacon Robinson finished his 15-minute presentation, he turned it back over to Pastor Marshall.

"Thank you, Deacon Robinson. Now, let's hear from Pastor Portis to hear his response to the report we just received from the deacon board," Pastor Marshall stated, calling Harold to the podium.

As he took his place, Harold said, "Thank you, Pastor Marshall, and thank all of you for coming out tonight. I know you are here because you love this church, as I do, and I am grateful for your support during my time here. Before you call for the vote tonight, my wife and I have prepared a statement that I would like to read to you that will make this evening's proceedings go a bit more smoothly and help the church move on and heal from the tumultuous weeks preceding this event."

Having said that, Harold read his prepared statement as the people sat in silence, listening to his resignation speech. It was obvious when Harold finished that Pastor Marshall, the deacons, and the congregation were not expecting to hear what Harold had just said. But that was nothing compared to the surprising events that were about to take place as Harold returned to his seat, fully expecting the meeting to close so he could get on with his life. Instead, something happened that people to this day say they had never seen or heard of before in a meeting such as was held that night at Three Rivers Baptist Church.

★★★★★

As Harold sat down, Pastor Marshall resumed his place as moderator at the microphone. "Well, that was not expected, but thank you, Pastor Portis, for your statement. I would assume that your resignation changes the course of this meeting, and that there is no need to proceed with a vote under these conditions." As Pastor Marshall said that, he looked over to where the deacons were seated, and saw them nod their agreement. It was then that the unexpected happened.

"Excuse me," said a woman's voice from the congregation. "Aren't you going to open things to the floor for comments and questions?" Harold looked and it was Sharlene's mother, Hazel, who was now standing after having broken the awkward silence.

There was a buzz of talk as people leaned over to comment to one another after Hazel had spoken. "Yes ma'am," Pastor Marshall said, "what is it that you would like to say?"

"May I come forward?" Hazel asked, everyone's eyes now riveted on her to see what would happen next. As they watched, Hazel got out of her pew and proceeded to the front. Pastor Marshall was surprised, but he moved out of the way to make room for Hazel at the microphone.

"Thank you, Pastor," Hazel began. "I have come to speak on behalf of many of us in the congregation who support Pastor Portis. We did not know that Pastor Portis would resign this evening, but we were and are here to stand with him for his courageous leadership during the past five years."

As Hazel said that, there was applause throughout the congregation, and Harold and Lois just looked at one another with a "What's going on?" look. Hazel continued.

"We feel that if there's anyone who should be voted on this evening, it would be our deacons who have engaged in what many of us consider to be a smear campaign against Pastor Portis," and as she spoke, Hazel looked directly at where the deacons were sitting.

"Tonight should not be a vote on our pastoral leadership. It should be a vote on the leadership of the church, our deacons, who seem devoted to keeping things as they are, not open to change in any way, shape, or form," Hazel stated surprising herself with her confidence and eloquence. As she stopped for affect, there was more applause, with many people nodding their heads in approval and declaring, "Amen!" or "That's right." The deacons sat in stunned silence, looking straight ahead and not at each other.

Hazel went on to describe many of the things that Pastor Portis had done that caused trouble for the leadership but not for her and others in the church. As she spoke, there was more applause and shouts of "Oh yes," and "You tell it" mingled in with Hazel's presentation.

She continued, "I was among those who was not happy, Pastor, and I let you know it. But last Sunday's message touched me and I am here to repent of my attitude. Forgive me, pastor and Mrs. Portis."

Harold and Lois looked at Hazel and nodded their

heads to accept her offer and extend forgiveness.

"Many of us don't blame you, Pastor Portis, for your decision tonight, and we will miss you." At that point, Sharlene approached her mother and whispered something in her ear. Hazel nodded in agreement and smiled, then said, "My daughter had an excellent idea. Pastor, while you are going to school, you will need a job, so why not continue to pastor here if the vote tonight is favorable toward keeping you? Would you consider that option?"

The meeting was in total turmoil as people stood, shouted, and applauded, as a few walked out. The deacons, Pastor Marshall, and Harold and Lois all tried to anticipate where things would end up, for they had entered uncharted territory and no one had any precedent to draw on to determine the way forward.

CHAPTER 9

Harold and Lois drove home from the meeting in total shock and disbelief at what they had just seen. Harold kept shaking his head slowly back and forth, occasionally saying, "Uh, uh, uh," while Lois just uttered, "Thank You, Lord, thank You, Lord" again and again.

"If I live to be 100," Harold said, "I'll never see anything like that again. What a night!"

Lois nodded, but she was still stuck declaring her ongoing mantra, "Thank You, Lord!'

After Hazel had spoken, a group of people approached Pastor Marshall, and then came to talk to Harold. They suggested that the vote continue as planned and, if the church voted to retain Pastor Portis, the group asked Harold and Lois if they would stay, knowing full well that he would pursue his purpose that included a doctor of ministry and then a teaching career.

Harold and Lois said they would stay but only if the people wanted them. With that, there was a motion from the floor that the vote proceed as planned. To Harold's utter amazement, the vote to retain him was 102 to 25. Harold had started the evening assuming he would be unemployed and heading toward being a full-time student. Instead, he had a job, a new purpose, and renewed faith in people and the power of God.

Then in a shocking turn of events, there was a motion from the floor to recall the deacons of the church who had spearheaded the recall movement. When that happened, Deacon Robinson and the others walked out of the church, and a unanimous voice vote was registered in favor of their removal. Harold and Lois then received a happy throng of well-wishers, including Sharlene and Harold's classmates from the seminary. Harold reached out to Pastor Marshall before he departed, asking him if he had ever witnessed anything like what had happened. Pastor Marshall had not, and then Harold asked him, "Where do we go from here?"

Pastor Marshall said, "Beats me. Let's talk later in the week after we see how the deacons respond, but I think you're going to need to elect some new deacons!" With that, they shook hands and Pastor Marshall headed home, as did Harold and Lois. Harold had begun to take things home from his church office, assuming his time was done, but as they exited the side door to their car, Harold smiled at the packed box on the chair by the door. He was going to take that box home with his personal effects from the office, but there would be no need to do that now.

Harold and Lois pulled into their driveway and garage, and as they entered the house, the children were up and waiting to hear what had happened. When their parents reported the news, both children applauded and with huge smiles on their faces, said to no one in particulate, "We don't have to move. The kids were wrong at church. We don't have to move!"

And with that, they all adjourned to the kitchen for a piece of blueberry pie that Lois had made, thinking she was going to have to cheer everyone up instead of hosting a celebration party. Again, she could only find it in her heart and mind to say, "Thank You, Jesus!"

★★★★★

The adrenaline was flowing and Harold knew that sleep was far off as he continued to process the evening's events. He watched some Sunday night football and then went down to his lounge chair devotional spot and opened to Psalm 26, another psalm that spoke to David's case for God to vindicate him:

Vindicate me, Lord,
for I have led a blameless life;
I have trusted in the Lord
and have not faltered.
Test me, Lord, and try me,

examine my heart and my mind;
for I have always been mindful of your unfailing love
and have lived in reliance on your faithfulness.

I do not sit with the deceitful,
nor do I associate with hypocrites.
I abhor the assembly of evildoers
and refuse to sit with the wicked.
I wash my hands in innocence,
and go about your altar, Lord,
proclaiming aloud your praise
and telling of all your wonderful deeds.

Lord, I love the house where you live,
the place where your glory dwells.
Do not take away my soul along with sinners,
my life with those who are bloodthirsty,
in whose hands are wicked schemes,
whose right hands are full of bribes.
I lead a blameless life;
deliver me and be merciful to me.

My feet stand on level ground;
in the great congregation I will praise the Lord.

Harold had never thought of vindication at Three Rivers, for it seemed that it was a foregone conclusion that he would be voted out of the pulpit. "Lord, You did indeed vindicate me tonight, and I am thankful," Harold prayed. "I do not take it to mean that I did everything correctly leading up to tonight's events, and I commit myself to be a better leader in the future." It was a little late to start a Bible study, but Harold went to his computer, opened his favorite Bible site, and typed in the word "enemies." He was surprised by how many references he found in the psalms where the writer prayed about or against his enemies, highlighting verses he wanted to take a closer look at in the morning:

- Lead me, Lord, in your righteousness because of my **enemies**—make your way straight before me (Psalm 5:8).

- All my **enemies** will be overwhelmed with shame and anguish; they will turn back and suddenly be put to shame (Psalm 6:10).

- Lord, see how my **enemies** persecute me! Have mercy and lift me up from the gates of death (Psalm 9:13).

- You prepare a table before me in the presence of my **enemies**. You anoint my head with oil; my cup overflows (Psalm 23:5).

- I trust in you; do not let me be put to shame, nor let my **enemies** triumph over me (Psalm 25:2).

- When the wicked advance against me to devour me, it is my **enemies** and my foes who will stumble and fall (Psalm 27:2).

- My times are in your hands; deliver me from the hands of my **enemies**, from those who pursue me (Psalm 31:15).

- Then my **enemies** will turn back when I call for help. By this I will know that God is for me (Psalm 56:9).

- The Lord is with me; he is my helper. I look in triumph on my **enemies** (Psalm 118:7).

- Rescue me from my **enemies**, Lord, for I hide myself in you (Psalm 143:9, emphasis added).

Harold was once again impressed that his enemies at the church had turned out to be his friends. They had performed a great service, for they caused him to seek the Lord like he had not sought Him before. They had caused him not just to sit in his class with Dr. Jackson to earn a grade, but forced him to pay attention to what the psalms were saying that so accurately addressed Harold's current realities. The process also allowed him to discover his purpose and future ministry path.

Harold had an enhanced appreciation for the role that Saul played in the development and composition of the psalms. Many of the references to enemies in the psalms were David's description of Saul and his army who were in constant pursuit of David to take his life. Without Saul, Harold realized, he would not have had so many meaningful things to read that pertained to his life. Without Saul, he would not have had the comfort and prayers of the psalms to lean on during his ordeal. Without Saul, David would not have pressed into the Lord and thus would not have provided Harold the model to do the same.

It was past 1 AM, but Harold was not tired. He was still energized by what had happened last night in church. He knew that 7 AM rolled around quickly, however, and that he took the children to school on Monday.

He left his Bible and journal open as he went upstairs for a few hours of sleep before he started his week as the born-again pastor of Three Rivers Baptist Church, something he did not expect to be as he went off to bed.

★★★★★

Lois called in sick the next morning, even though she was more tired and emotionally drained than sick. After Harold returned from dropping off the children at school, Lois was awake and waiting for him to discuss the previous evening's events.

"Well, the children were certainly thrilled when I told them how last night went," Lois reported. "I think it was affecting them more than they let on."

"Yes, they were telling me in the car that they thought we were going to move, and maybe go back to Buffalo, which didn't excite them," Harold added. "It's a big relief for all of us, isn't it?"

"Sure is," Lois responded, "but I could hardly sleep last night as I thought about how the evening unfolded."

"Yeah, me too," Harold said, "and I almost stayed up even later to continue my study of Psalms in light of what happened."

"Sounds like a school lesson is in order," Lois said smiling. "Meet you at the kitchen table for coffee."

"Is it too early for pie?" Harold inquired.

"Yes, but it won't be when we finish," Lois said as she headed to the kitchen, while Harold retrieved his materials from the basement.

★★★★★

Harold and Lois spent their morning praying, thanking God for His deliverance and help, and looking into the Scriptures. They especially prayed for the deacons at Three Rivers and that the church would heal from this latest dilemma and move on to be a church and not a battleground. During this morning session, Lois was the first to offer her insight.

"I've been so impacted by our study of Psalms," Lois began, "and I'd been praying my own psalm during this ordeal that I found one morning after our Thursday night discussion. It's Psalm 143."

Lord, hear my prayer,
listen to my cry for mercy;
in your faithfulness and righteousness
come to my relief.
Do not bring your servant into judgment,
for no one living is righteous before you.
The enemy pursues me,
he crushes me to the ground;
he makes me dwell in the darkness
like those long dead.
So my spirit grows faint within me;
my heart within me is dismayed.
I remember the days of long ago;
I meditate on all your works
and consider what your hands have done.
I spread out my hands to you;
I thirst for you like a parched land.

Answer me quickly, Lord;

my spirit fails.
Do not hide your face from me
or I will be like those who go down to the pit.
Let the morning bring me word of your unfailing love,
for I have put my trust in you.
Show me the way I should go,
for to you I entrust my life.
Rescue me from my enemies, Lord,
for I hide myself in you.
Teach me to do your will,
for you are my God;
may your good Spirit
lead me on level ground.

For your name's sake, Lord, preserve my life;
in your righteousness, bring me out of trouble.
In your unfailing love, silence my enemies;
destroy all my foes,
for I am your servant.

"You know what we haven't done in a few weeks?" Harold said after Lois finished. "We haven't used our six questions that help analyze the psalm. Let's do that with Psalm 143."

1. Who is speaking in the psalm? They both agreed that this psalm belonged to David.

2. Is this psalm personal or corporate? This psalm was personal, for David was crying to the Lord for help, not for the nation or the people, but for himself!

3. For what purpose was the psalm written? This psalm was written because David was in serious trouble and, unless the Lord delivered him, he was going to perish. David was asking God to deal with his enemies who had put him in a difficult place.

4. What was the emotional orientation of the psalm? There is an urgency and anxiety in what David was praying. He was depressed and downtrodden because of the work of his enemies and he was specific as he reported to God the condition of his heart and emotions.

5. What is the genre? This is a psalm that contains a prayer of confidence, although it is also a lament as David poured out his heart to the Lord because of the work of his enemies.

6. Is there a recurring refrain or words in the psalm? There are none, but there is a recurring word and that is enemy, enemies, and foes.

"I prayed that psalm every day leading up to last night," Lois added. "But even today, I'm seeing new things I hadn't previously noticed. For instance, David prayed 'Show me the way I should go,' and he was counting on God directing his steps so that he could avoid his enemies. Last night, God showed us the way we should go. He made a way where there seemed no way!"

"That's good insight, honey, and God it's obvious that God answered your prayer," Harold said. "I was more focused on the concept of vindication last night. You know I had been repenting for my attitudes and actions, and I'd lost focus on the fact that God had directed me to do some of the things I did – like moving the altar."

Harold then looked up the definition of

vindication: "the action of clearing someone of blame or suspicion." Harold then did an online search to see what the Bible had to say about vindication.

- Let the Lord judge the peoples. **Vindicate** me, Lord, according to my righteousness, according to my integrity, O Most High (Psalm 7:8).

- As for me, I will be **vindicate**d and will see your face; when I awake, I will be satisfied with seeing your likeness (Psalm 17:15).

- **Vindicate** me, Lord, for I have led a blameless life; I have trusted in the Lord and have not faltered (Psalm 26:1).

- **Vindicate** me in your righteousness, Lord my God; do not let them gloat over me (Psalm 35:24).

- **Vindicate** me, my God, and plead my cause against an unfaithful nation. Rescue me from those who are deceitful and wicked (Psalm 43:1).

- Save me, O God, by your name; **vindicate** me by your might (Psalm 54:1).

- I cry out to God Most High, to God, who **vindicate**s me (Psalm 57:2).

- For the Lord will **vindicate** his people and have compassion on his servants (Psalm 135:14).

- The Lord will **vindicate** me; your love,

Lord, endures forever—do not abandon the works of your hands (Psalm 138:8, emphasis added).

"I see now that I was so focused on my own shortcomings that I never prayed for God's will to be done in the congregation regarding the changes I had instituted," Harold reflected. "My enemies put me on the defensive and I was backtracking instead of moving forward!"

Lois and Harold shared more thoughts and reflections, prayed some more, thanked God some more, and then they had the pie that had been promised, for as Lois suspected, it was late morning when they finished.

"What are you up to for the rest of the day?" Lois asked.

"I have a paper due for Thursday's class, and in this one, I want to examine the contrast between the righteous and the wicked in the book of psalms."

"Sounds good," Lois said enthusiastically. "I can't wait to read it. But I'm going back to bed to rest before the kids get home."

CHAPTER 10

The week went by quickly for Harold and there were more surprises in store for him as the events of Sunday night's meeting played out. He received many texts and emails supporting him and expressing happiness that he would be staying on as pastor. Harold did not quite know what would happen with the deacons, but he received several resignations but a few requested meetings with him to explain that they were caught up in the opposition movement but regretted their role.

Harold worked throughout the week on his paper for class, both looking forward to the class being over while regretting that it was almost done. He had learned so much about the psalms, about himself, and about the Lord and he knew this class would go down as one of his all-time favorites.

The focus of Harold's prayer and devotional life changed after the meeting, and he entered into another common theme of the psalms that have been enjoyed by millions through the ages and that is praise. His morning devotional times were transformed from times when Harold poured out his heart in pain to times of praise and worship!

Harold had learned in class that the collection of psalms ended with profuse praise to God. The final five psalms were dedicated to praise without petitions or lament:

Psalm 146

Praise the Lord.

Praise the Lord, my soul.

I will praise the Lord all my life;
I will sing praise to my God as long as I live.
Do not put your trust in princes,
in human beings, who cannot save.
When their spirit departs, they return to the ground;
on that very day their plans come to nothing.
Blessed are those whose help is the God of Jacob,
whose hope is in the Lord their God.

He is the Maker of heaven and earth,
the sea, and everything in them—
he remains faithful forever.
He upholds the cause of the oppressed

and gives food to the hungry.
The Lord sets prisoners free,
the Lord gives sight to the blind,
the Lord lifts up those who are bowed down,
the Lord loves the righteous.
The Lord watches over the foreigner
and sustains the fatherless and the widow,
but he frustrates the ways of the wicked.

The Lord reigns forever,
your God, O Zion, for all generations.

Praise the Lord.

The way the psalms ended suddenly made more sense to Harold. After the first 144 psalms had traversed the entire emotional repertoire of human existence – joy, sorrow, disappointment, frustration, depression, and anger – the editors summed up man's ultimate reason for existence and that was to praise the Lord. Harold also realized that the praise was not for God's sake; He was not insecure or in need of flattery. The need to praise was how man had originally been created, and it was the summation of man's highest purpose as summarized by the Westminster Confession:

Question: What is the chief end of man?
Answer: Man's chief end is to glorify God, and to enjoy him forever.

Harold also spent some time studying Psalm 149:

Praise the Lord.
Sing to the Lord a new song,
his praise in the assembly of his faithful people.

Let Israel rejoice in their Maker;
let the people of Zion be glad in their King.
Let them praise his name with dancing
and make music to him with timbrel and harp.
For the Lord takes delight in his people;
he crowns the humble with victory.
Let his faithful people rejoice in this honor
and sing for joy on their beds.

May the praise of God be in their mouths
and a double-edged sword in their hands,
to inflict vengeance on the nations
and punishment on the peoples,
to bind their kings with fetters,
their nobles with shackles of iron,
to carry out the sentence written against them—
this is the glory of all his faithful people.

Praise the Lord.

Harold saw how much of a diversion his recent squabble with the deacons had been, for it redirected the attention and energy of the church away from its mission in favor of internal affairs. Harold realized that Jesus had given His marching orders to the church in Matthew 28:18-20, which seemed to coincide with Psalm 148:6-9. Harold spent the week reflecting on the Great Commission in Matthew 28:18-20 and vowed never again to devote so much energy to anything but spreading the gospel and directives of God's kingdom to as many people as possible:

Then Jesus came to them and said, "All authority in

heaven and on earth has been given to me. Therefore go and make disciples of all nations, baptizing them in the name of the Father and of the Son and of the Holy Spirit, and teaching them to obey everything I have commanded you. And surely I am with you always, to the very end of the age."

Most of Harold's week, however, was devoted to his final paper and when Thursday arrived, as it always did, Harold was busy putting the finishing touches on his work right up to the time he headed to class. Little did he realize that even more surprises awaited him there in what had turned out to be a week full of the unexpected.

★★★★★

Before he went to class, Harold stopped by the church office to print out his paper. Mildred was not there but they had talked by phone, with Mildred expressing a need to sit down and talk to discuss her future. Harold promised Mildred they would talk next week after he got through class and the weekend. Harold did ask Mildred to get him Hazel Fuller's number, for he wanted to call and thank her for her role in Sunday night's meeting.

Harold went into his office, sent his paper to the printer, and then looked at a letter with a handwritten address and no return address. He jokingly thought that perhaps he should have the letter scanned for explosives, but went ahead and opened it. Inside he found a note and it was signed by Deacon Washington:

Pastor Portis,

I hereby submit my resignation as deacon of Three Rivers Baptist Church.

Sincerely,

Melvin Washington

Well, that was short and sweet, Harold thought. *I wonder where the rest of the deacons stand?*

With paper in hand, Harold set off for the seminary. When he arrived, most of the close-by parking spaces were taken, so he had to park at a distance and run for class. When he got to the classroom, the students all jumped to their feet and cheered wildly.

"Praise the Lord, thank You, Jesus, Hallelujah" rang out in the classroom as Harold's peers and his professor stood and applauded. When it subsided, Dr. Jackson said, "Sharlene and the others gave us a full update on your situation, Harold, and we're all delighted for you that it went so well."

With that, the students applauded again. Harold was surprised, and he could not hold back a tear or two, remembering God's faithfulness of having Harold in this class on the psalms at this point in his life and ministry.

"Thank you, all," Harold finally managed to say, "your prayers made all the difference. And Sharlene, I know you had a hand in what your mother did on our behalf Sunday night. Thank you too, and thanks to all of you who came out to support me on Sunday." The class applauded one more time, acknowledging all that Harold had said.

Then Dr. Jackson chimed in and said, "Well, Pastor Portis, I have one more surprise for you, but that will have to wait until the break when we can talk since class is ready to begin." Everyone sat down and half of the students began to make their 20-minute presentations that summarized the theme of their papers, highlighting what they had learned in class (the other six were scheduled to present next week in the final class). Harold was glad that they had drawn numbers to determine the order of their presentation and he calculated he would not have to present until after the break.

Dr. Jackson took his seat in the back of the room, and Sharlene was the first to present her paper. Here are the notes that Harold took as she spoke:

Speaker: Sharlene

Topic: The Psalms as a Prayer Guide

Insights: Many of the psalms are prayers. Therefore, we should pray them as often as possible for ourselves and for others. (Harold had already discovered this in the time leading up to his Sunday night surprise meeting). The psalms cover the entirety of human emotion — joy, sorrow, anxiety, fear, peace, anger. Therefore, we can approach God as we are, and not pretending to be something or someplace that we are not.

The psalms were prayers that were recorded, not just spoken. Therefore, our own personal journals should include our prayers as we pray them. Since David and the psalmists shared their prayers, perhaps we should share ours in some format (social media, preaching, Bible studies) to teach others how to pray.

Some have considered Psalms the hymnbook of Israel but it was Sharlene's opinion that it was Israel's prayer book.

Speaker: Martin

Topic: The Ultimate Lesson for Israel

Insights: The psalms were edited and compiled in Babylon in the sixth century BC. By then, most of the psalms were six centuries old and some were more than 1,000 years old. In Babylon, Israel had lost everything they held dear: their land, their Temple, and their national identity as a people. It was during this time that the Jews developed and instituted the synagogue as a focus for worship gatherings. What's more, the psalms end with a barrage of praise and worship psalms. The Jews recognized while in Babylon, stripped of all they held dear, that they still had two things upon which they could come together as a people: The Law and worship of the one true God. That is the ultimate lesson of the psalms! God and His word are the people of God's most valuable possessions!

Speaker: Pamela

Topic: Jesus in the Psalms

Insights: The entire Old Testament points to the coming of Christ. Jesus said in Luke 24:44: "This is what I told you while I was still with you: Everything must be fulfilled that is written about me in the Law of Moses, the Prophets and the Psalms." Jesus used the psalms to explain His mission and purpose. Therefore, we should read the psalms not just with an eye toward what they can provide for us, but for what they can tell us to enhance our understanding and appreciation for Jesus.

Harold had miscalculated, so he was the last to present before the break.

Topic: The Contrast Between the Righteous and the Wicked in the Psalms

Insights: There are two categories of people who are discussed in the Psalms. They are the righteous – those who put their trust in the Lord – and the wicked – those who do not. Psalm 1 introduces these two groups and the remainder of the book discusses the practices of both groups. The righteous are totally dependent upon the Lord. The wicked are too powerful and numerous for the righteous to overcome in their own strength. The righteous are poor, oppressed, downtrodden, and can only look to the Lord for their survival. At times, they are overwhelmed by the wicked.

The wicked are self-reliant and self-sufficient,

so they take matters into their own hands by scheming and using and abusing power to get what they want and need. Therefore, they mistreat the righteous who can only look to God for their salvation and deliverance. This salvation, however, is not always forthcoming, so it appears the wicked have the upper hand while God's people suffer.

As the righteous come to God for help, they must face their own inadequacies and sins, and must confess them to God while they also call out for mercy and help. They do this through a passionate prayer life, and their encounters with God do not end with their circumstances changing but rather with praise and worship for who God is and not necessarily for what He has done – for the wicked may continue to oppress them.

Throughout the psalms, the people speak to God but then God actually speaks to them in the first person, as found in Psalm 81:

> *Sing for joy to God our strength;*
> *shout aloud to the God of Jacob!*
> *Begin the music, strike the timbrel,*
> *play the melodious harp and lyre.*
> *Sound the ram's horn at the New Moon,*
> *and when the moon is full, on the day of our festival;*
> *this is a decree for Israel,*
> *an ordinance of the God of Jacob.*

When God went out against Egypt,
he established it as a statute for Joseph.
I heard an unknown voice say:
"I removed the burden from their shoulders;
their hands were set free from the basket.
In your distress you called and I rescued you,
I answered you out of a thundercloud;
I tested you at the waters of Meribah.
Hear me, my people, and I will warn you—
if you would only listen to me, Israel!
You shall have no foreign god among you;
you shall not worship any god other than me.
I am the Lord your God,
who brought you up out of Egypt.
Open wide your mouth and I will fill it.

"But my people would not listen to me;
Israel would not submit to me.
So I gave them over to their stubborn hearts
to follow their own devices.

"If my people would only listen to me,
if Israel would only follow my ways,
how quickly I would subdue their enemies
and turn my hand against their foes!
Those who hate the Lord would cringe before him,
and their punishment would last forever.
But you would be fed with the finest of wheat;
with honey from the rock I would satisfy you."

God actually spoke to His people in Psalm 81,
but He promised to deliver them only when

they made a commitment to follow His ways and obey His commands.

Conclusion: The righteous align with God while the wicked do not. Therefore, the righteous seek to act as God would have them act, even though conditions may be difficult or unfair. The righteous conclude that the Lord reigns, even though it may seem like He is distant and unconcerned. The righteous' focus is therefore on God, while the wicked focus on themselves and their own desires, conspiring to do whatever is necessary to serve their own purposes.

When Harold had finished, the class adjourned for fifteen minutes. Dr. Jackson had wanted to speak to Harold, but he was preoccupied with some of the other students, and Harold was fine with waiting till the end of class to talk with him.

As Harold listened to his classmates make their presentations, he was once again impressed with the diversity of insight into the psalms. Most of the class presented material that Harold had never considered before. He thought, *I will have to remember to use this exercise and have the students help teach the class when I am a professor.* Harold took a lot of notes for his post-class debrief with Lois.

When Harold talked with Dr. Jackson after class, he received even more to report to Lois. He raced home after class to tell her the good news.

★★★★★

Harold came up from the garage after he got home, and there on the table was a piece of apple pie waiting for him. "Do you want some ice cream with that?" Lois asked.

"Ice cream? No, I want champagne. Wait, we're Baptist, so I want sparkling grape juice! We need to celebrate more good news," Harold said as he picked Lois up and spun her around. "What a week this has been, a glorious week!" Harold continued, with Lois still in the dark as to why her husband was so exuberant.

Lois was bewildered and tried to determine Harold's reason for such jubilation. "Did you get an A on your paper?" Lois guessed.

"No, it's bigger and better than that. Sit down and let me tell you," Harold said, more anxious to tell Lois than he was to eat his pie – unusual behavior for Harold.

"After class tonight, Dr. Jackson wanted to speak with me," Harold began. "He knew about the meeting last week and that it was possibly my last week at the church. He explained that he was searching for a graduate assistant who would qualify for a scholarship under the Old Testament studies chair at the seminary, and he offered me the position! Isn't that great?"

"Yes, I suppose," Lois answered, "but what does that mean?"

"What does it mean?" Harold echoed. "It means that they will pay the rest of my tuition and give me a stipend to go with it. It means that I get to assist Dr. Jackson in researching and writing his next book."

"But what about the church?" Lois asked, still not ready to celebrate, assuming there was some drawback or catch.

"Dr. Jackson had assumed that I would be out of a job when he considered me for the position, but he said tonight that he didn't see why I could not be his assistant and pastor at the same time," Harold added as he got up to stand by the kitchen sink. "Tuition paid, a monthly stipend, a chance to do research, and time to learn from Dr. Jackson to fulfill my purpose of teaching at the graduate level."

"What's more, Dr. Jackson believed that this would extend through my Doctor of Ministry studies as well!" Harold said in a loud voice.

"Ssshhhh," Lois cautioned, "the children are sleeping."

"I can't be quiet, Lois," Harold responded, "What a week, what a magnificent week!" With that, Harold sat down to eat his pie and it was then Lois' turn to express her joy.

"Harold, I'm so proud of you, but you know that this is the Lord's doing," and with that, Lois began to thank the Lord with eyes closed, standing on her feet, rocking to and fro.

"Yes," Harold said, "it's the Lord! This week is ending like the psalms ended – with praise and worship." With that, Harold got his Bible out of his briefcase and turned to Psalm 150, the last psalm. He sat down and Lois sat on his lap so they could read this final psalm out loud together:

Praise the Lord.

Praise God in his sanctuary;
praise him in his mighty heavens.
Praise him for his acts of power;
praise him for his surpassing greatness.
Praise him with the sounding of the trumpet,
praise him with the harp and lyre,
praise him with timbrel and dancing,
praise him with the strings and pipe,
praise him with the clash of cymbals,
praise him with resounding cymbals.

Let everything that has breath praise the Lord.

Praise the Lord.

And with those praise-filled words, Harold finished his pie, got out his notes from the evening's class, and prepared to share with Lois what he learned from his classmates, knowing that the study of the psalms that had begun just a few weeks ago would undoubtedly continue for the rest of their lives.

A WORD FROM THE AUTHOR

If you are like me, you treasure the book of Psalms and have used it over the years to comfort and console you, to find words of praise that often escape you, or to read King David's brutally honest prayers against his enemies – prayers you hesitate to pray yourself and sometimes wish were not in the Bible.

As Harold Portis explained, the book of Psalms is like a box of chocolates with many flavors and shapes. If we know what are looking for in the psalms, we can pick out what we want and ignore the rest, leaving them for someone else to consume according to their need or taste.

Until just a few years ago, I treated Psalms like the candy. I went in and used my finger to push aside what I didn't like until I found what I was looking for. I consumed it and then moved on. Yes, I read the Psalms when I read through the Bible, and even followed someone's advice to read five psalms every day, which enabled me to read through all 150 psalms in a month. I sang the psalms and listened to teaching on the psalms, but until I personally taught the psalms, I never really understood the book as a whole.

The chance to teach came in 2014 when I was a part-time faculty member for Geneva College at the Center for Urban Biblical Ministry in Pittsburgh, PA. The program in which I taught was for adults who were coming back to school, often being away from academia for decades, to earn an associate degree in Christian ministry, leadership, or human services. I taught the leadership classes, but was asked to teach many of the Bible classes because I had earned my Doctor of Ministry. Over the years, I taught Acts, Paul's epistles, Romans, Revelation, and the non-Pauline epistles, just to name a few. Those classes were beneficial to me in my writing, preaching, and ministry, but teaching the book of Psalms impacted my life like the other courses had not.

My initial plan was to teach the psalms by reading each one of them, one by one, in class and discussing them. I had planned on paying attention to the headings where they existed and then studying the historical context to better understand the psalm itself. I did some of that (we didn't read every psalm), but as I began to research and study the psalms as a unit, I was moved and impacted by what I found. That class and topic became my all-time favorite, and as I write, I am teaching it again.

I immediately began to think about how I could share what I had learned with others who were not in the class, but did not feel like I could do a commentary, since my Hebrew studies are not very comprehensive. Then in 2017, I published my first fiction work, a leadership fable that taught leadership truths, and shortly thereafter, Pastor Harold Portis came into being – at least on the pages of *My Enemies My Friends*.

I have been in church work all my adult life, 40-plus years as I write. I have seen the good, the bad, and the ugly. Pastor Portis is a combination of things I have witnessed along with a heavy dose of fantasy where a potential church tragedy has a happy ending – except for Mildred and the deacons. Unfortunately, those happy endings don't happen often enough, and frequently those who leaders and members believe are their friends turn out to be fickle or downright mean. But the story of *My Enemies My Friends* is simply the vehicle to deliver the payload of insight from the psalms that has changed the way I read and teach them.

There are so many significant takeaways from the class I taught, but the one that was most profound for me was the fact that not only are the psalms the inspired word of God, but so is their order. I thought the 150 psalms were a loosely-knit collection of poems, hymns, and prayers related by the fact that David wrote many of them (73 to be exact) while some priests in charge of corporate worship composed most of the remainder.

I had no idea that the editors who put the order of psalms together had a purpose in the work they did. They took a psalm that Moses wrote in 1300 BC, added it to the 73 that David wrote, added one that Solomon, David's son, wrote and chose psalms composed by the sons of Korah, Heman, and Asaph to put a book together that told a story about God's people and their journey with Him. The story of the book was one of failure, denial, suffering, redemption, insight, revelation, prayer, praise, worship, triumph, and grace.

The psalms were compiled sometime after the Babylonians carried the Jews off into exile in 587 BC under the leadership of the notorious and foul-tempered Nebuchadnezzar. If someone got on that king's wrong side, they found their house an ash heap, often with them and their family still in it! The Jews were confident God would *never* turn them over to a Gentile leader like Nebuchadnezzar because, after all, they were God's covenant people. They had the Torah, the Temple, the promises of God, and were responsible for the animal sacrificial system – and God *needed* those sacrifices, or so they thought.

Jeremiah repeatedly warned them that their exile was nigh, but they mocked, ignored, arrested, and belittled him. When Jeremiah's word came true, it was total devastation for Judah, their homeland, as well as the Temple. Nebuchadnezzar carried the gold and silver utensils from the Temple to Babylon, along with many of the survivors of his siege. Suddenly people who once had a nation and a national way of life that centered around the Temple and holy assemblies had nothing.

Those taken into exile took little with them, but somehow some of them took the Torah and the psalms. When they got to Babylon, they met together to try and make sense of what had happened. That's when the editors, and we have no idea who they were, began to put the individual psalms in an order that sent a message and told a story of where Israel had been and who they truly were as a people. They came to conclusions about what was to have been most important to them – the Law and true worship – but had been obscured as they built a religious system that preserved their traditions instead of honoring God.

Why did this order show me that changed my

life? It showed me that the creativity of the editors was as inspired as those who wrote the psalms. Their editorial decisions were vital to the Psalms' message and the editing I was doing on my own books and those of others (I had started a publishing company in 2014) was not just to make sure the punctuation and spelling were correct, but to ensure that the book flowed together to send the message the authors intended. I was set free to not only be an author but also an editor, and to see those two roles as equally important. You may read the last sentence and conclude, "that's not a big deal," but to me it was just that: a big deal.

Harold Portis found out that the five books into which the psalms are divided were there for a reason. The editors concluded, rightly so, that before there was a Temple or a tabernacle or a Promised Land or a priesthood, God had revealed Himself to His people through His word, the first five books of the Bible written by Moses and referred to as the Pentateuch or the Torah (the Law). Therefore, the five books in the psalms were a message to the survivors in Babylon, those who returned to the land, and for God's people forevermore that the word of God was the solid foundation, the rock upon which God's people would stand. The Word was their identify and it was the most precious possession the people had. They could lose the Temple, their land, and their priesthood, but they still had what was most important – God's revealed will through His word.

But that's not all. The five books each have a message, but they also led to another conclusion contained in the last five psalms, 146 through 150. Those psalms contain only one message: People are to praise the Lord! In addition to the Word or Torah, the Jews were to be a people of exuberant, lavish, verbal, regular, and musical praise. They could worship and praise anywhere and everywhere, which is why they established the synagogue system while they were in Babylon to replace the Temple worship they lost. They took the synagogue custom back with them to their homeland after the exile was over, and today our churches are modeled after what happened in the synagogue: worship and the reading and teaching of the Word.

I have walked you through the 150 psalms to their conclusion but forgive me, for I was out of order. I need to take you back to the first two psalms, for they reinforce what I have already written, but they also introduce another important theme. Psalm 1 simply contrasts two categories of people: the righteous and the evil. The righteous are those who base their life on the word of God, and the evil do not. Simple enough and that truth is consistent with what I have already told you.

Psalm 2 introduced another theme. The Jews had not only lost their homeland, their Temple, their national identity, and their way of life; they had also lost their king. That may not have been significant to other people, but the Jews had received a promise through David that one of his sons would always reign on David's throne. That was another reason why the Jews were confident that God would never take them into exile. If that happened, how would the promise of David's sons on the throne be fulfilled? Furthermore, the Jews thought that the promise was for a political king. When they were carried off to Babylon, one author summarized it as a crisis in the monarchy.

The editors examined that promise to David's descendants, however, and came to another conclusion. They realized the promise was still in effect, but the king was not to be a political one, but a spiritual one. The Jews were still the keepers and protectors of the promise that the Messiah would come from among them and rule the nations. That truth was what Psalm 2 was addressing:

> *Why do the nations conspire*
> *and the peoples plot in vain?*
> *The kings of the earth rise up*
> *and the rulers band together*
> *against the Lord and against his anointed, saying,*
> *"Let us break their chains*
> *and throw off their shackles."*
>
> *The One enthroned in heaven laughs;*
> *the Lord scoffs at them.*
> *He rebukes them in his anger*
> *and terrifies them in his wrath, saying,*
> *"I have installed my king*
> *on Zion, my holy mountain."*
>
> *I will proclaim the Lord's decree:*
>
> *He said to me, "You are my son;*
> *today I have become your father.*
> *Ask me,*
> *and I will make the nations your inheritance,*

the ends of the earth your possession.
You will break them with a rod of iron;
you will dash them to pieces like pottery."

Therefore, you kings, be wise;
be warned, you rulers of the earth.
Serve the Lord with fear
and celebrate his rule with trembling.
Kiss his son, or he will be angry
and your way will lead to your destruction,
for his wrath can flare up in a moment.
Blessed are all who take refuge in him.

From that psalm, the book directed the attention of the readers to what was yet to come – the son of David, God's son, who would rule His enemies with an iron hand, but His people with a shepherd's heart. Therefore, the psalms were and are about Jesus, and Jesus Himself explained to the disciples when psalms spoke about Him and how He fulfilled their words. The New Testament is full of references to the psalms and we can rest assured that those explanations and applications were handed to the disciples by Jesus Himself.

Let's return to the five books of Psalms. Each one had a theme, as Harold Portis discovered and shared with Lois. They traced the gradual realization of the Jews in exile that they had indeed caused the exile, and that God had been faithful to preserve them despite their waywardness. The fifth book includes 15 psalms called the psalms of ascents that pilgrims were to recite as they went up (Jews always went "up" to Jerusalem, no matter the direction of their approach). If the Jews were never going back to their land, then why preserve those psalms? The truth is that the people in exile knew they were going back, and the message the editors were telling was that when they got back home, they would be wiser and more obedient. They would keep first things first and the main thing the main thing.

The Jews did go home but soon they returned to their futile efforts to build a nation centered around the Temple and the priesthood. They became so proficient and efficient that when Jesus came, the King who was the focus of Psalm 2, they rejected and killed Him. Yet that had been predicted in the psalms, including the role of Judas, Jesus' betrayer:

> *All my enemies whisper together against me;*
> *they imagine the worst for me, saying,*
> *"A vile disease has afflicted him;*
> *he will never get up from the place where he lies."*
> *Even my close friend,*
> *someone I trusted,*
> *one who shared my bread,*
> *has turned against me (Psalm 41:7-9).*

Harold and Lois Portis discovered more about the psalms than they previously realized was there because they had to do so. They were about to be ousted from their church, or so they thought, and some of their friends turned out to be enemies. Yet those enemies were really their friends, for they helped them discover the deeper message in the book of Psalms as one book and not only a collection of individual parts. They saw the role that Saul played in the development of David and the psalms he produced, which gave them a whole new perspective on the crisis they were facing at Three Rivers Baptist.

As I bring this project to a close, I hope you have enjoyed the story and have learned something about the book of Psalms you did not know. Even so, that is not what I hope will be your main takeaway from this book. I hope you are now able to approach the psalms in a new way that will enhance your appreciation for the book and improve your ability to use it as a prayer book, worship tool, and life guide. I hope you will appreciate the creativity of the psalmists along with the editors who decided its order to send a message to help describe their journey.

It's appropriate to end this book with nothing else but a psalm and what better psalm to use than the best-known psalm of all, Psalm 23:

The Lord is my shepherd, I lack nothing.
He makes me lie down in green pastures,
he leads me beside quiet waters,
he refreshes my soul.
He guides me along the right paths
for his name's sake.
Even though I walk
through the darkest valley,
I will fear no evil,
for you are with me;
your rod and your staff,
they comfort me.

You prepare a table before me

in the presence of my enemies.
You anoint my head with oil;
my cup overflows.
Surely your goodness and love will follow me
all the days of my life,
and I will dwell in the house of the Lord forever.

Amen.

ABOUT THE AUTHOR

John Stanko was born in Pittsburgh, Pennsylvania. After graduating from St. Basil's Prep School in Stamford, Connecticut, he attended Duquesne University where he received his bachelor's and master's degrees in economics in 1972 and 1974 respectively.

Since then, John has served as an administrator, teacher, consultant, author, and pastor in his professional career. He holds a second master's degree in pastoral ministries, and earned his doctorate in pastoral ministries from Liberty Theological Seminary in Houston, Texas in 1995. He recently completed a second doctor of ministry degree at Reformed Presbyterian Theological Seminary in Pittsburgh.

John has taught extensively on the topics of time management, life purpose and organization, and has conducted leadership and purpose training sessions throughout the United States and in 32 countries. He is also certified to administer the DISC and other related personality assessments as well as the Natural Church Development profile for churches. In 2006, he earned the privilege to facilitate for The Pacific Institute of Seattle, a leadership and personal development program, and for The Leadership Circle, a provider of cultural and executive 360-degree profiles. He has authored fifteen books and written for many publications around the world.

John founded a personal and leadership development company, called PurposeQuest, in 2001 and today travels the world to speak, consult and inspire leaders and people everywhere. From 2001–2008, he spent six months a year in Africa and still enjoys visiting and working on that continent, while teaching for Geneva College's Masters of Organizational Leadership and the Center for Urban Biblical Ministry in his hometown of Pittsburgh, Pennsylvania. John has been married for 38 years to Kathryn Scimone Stanko, and they have two adult children. In 2009, John was appointed the administrative pastor for discipleship at Allegheny Center Alliance Church on the North Side of Pittsburgh where he served for five years. Most recently, John founded Urban Press, a publishing service designed to tell stories of the city, from the city and to the city.

KEEP IN TOUCH
WITH JOHN STANKO

www.purposequest.com

www.johnstanko.us

www.stankobiblestudy.com

www.stankomondaymemo.com

or via email at johnstanko@gmail.com

John also does extensive relief and community development work in Kenya. You can see some of his projects at
www.purposequest.com/contributions

PurposeQuest International
PO Box 8882
Pittsburgh, PA 15221-0882

ADDITIONAL TITLES BY JOHN STANKO

A Daily Dose of Proverbs

A Daily Taste of Proverbs

A String of Pearls

Changing the Way We Do Church

I Wrote This Book on Purpose

Life Is A Gold Mine: Can You Dig It?

Strictly Business

The Faith Files, Volume 1

The Faith Files, Volume 2

The Faith Files, Volume 3

The Leadership Walk

The Price of Leadership

Unlocking the Power of Your Creativity

Unlocking the Power of Your Productivity

Unlocking the Power of Your Purpose

Unlocking the Power of You

What Would Jesus Ask You Today?

Your Life Matters